ABOUT T]

DAVID SCOTT COWAN graduated from the University of Aberdeen in English Literature and was for many years a television producer in BBC Education. He now devotes much of his time to architectural research and family history. He is married and lives in East Sussex.

THE LADY IN BLUE

For Lorne,

David Scott Cowan

DAVID SCOTT COWAN

First published in Great Britain by David Scott Cowan 2021

Paperback ISBN 978-1-913663-77-3

Typeset in Palatino Linotype
Cover design by Kevin Moore

Printed in England by
Biddles Books Ltd.
Castle House
East Winch Rd
Blackborough End
King's Lynn PE32 1SF

For Carol and Alex

PROLOGUE

The Present

"Dammit." Rosemary Nugent, lecturer in Law, was not given to strong language, but this was really too much. Her brand-new Fiat 500 was stubbornly unresponsive to her repeated attempts to start it. It was no good; there was no point in persisting. She got out and stared at it, pondering the options for keeping her day on track.

"Having problems, Rosemary?"

"Oh Alexis, thank heavens you're here. I hardly dare ask, but you couldn't possibly give me a lift down to the Law College, could you? I can't start my car – it's completely dead."

"If you can give me five minutes to make a couple of calls, I'll be all yours." Alexis Tobin, estate agent and sales representative, was effectively Rosemary's next door neighbour: Number One, Ferndown Close was the show house for the newly completed development. Rosemary's house, Number Thirteen, was the last in sequence around the tangle of cul-de-sacs that made up the estate and stood next door to the first. But now that most of the houses were sold, Alexis was less frequently on site.

"That's so kind of you. I was going to stop by the supermarket on the way, so I've got half an hour if you need it."

"Right. Time for a quick coffee then. Come in and sit down." Alexis busied herself in the small kitchen of the show house while speaking rapidly into her mobile, adjusting her diary to accommodate Rosemary's predicament. Though the two were both busy professionals, their paths had crossed often enough for Rosemary to consider Alexis a friend and, moreover, one who had the gift of being a good listener. In the weeks since Rosemary had moved in, Alexis had lent a sympathetic ear to the domestic drama that comprised her neighbour's life: her messy divorce from Ian; the trauma of the sale of the big house in Wonersh; her worries at the prospect of early retirement; her delight at becoming a grandmother, even though her son had settled in Australia and she could barely afford to visit.

"Here you go. Milk and sugar on the counter."

"Thanks, you're an angel. You've been so kind to me; I shall miss you."

"Nonsense, it's what we're here for. And I needed to go into Weyford anyway."

"How much more do you have to do here?"

"Still a few loose ends to tidy up. You haven't quite seen the last of me." Alexis smiled. She leant forward, her eyes looking up into Rosemary's, her expression reassuring and engaging. For a moment there was a pause. Rosemary broke the slightly awkward silence.

"I love your necklace."

"Thank you. It is pretty, isn't it?"

The young estate agent was wearing a crisp white shirt which set off a fine gold chain in the form of a snake. The clasp was formed by the snake's mouth swallowing its tail. The snake's head was picked out in turquoise, and its body was made of intricately interlocking links representing the scales.

"It's called Ouroboros. It's a design from antiquity."

"Very unusual."

"Yes. It was given to me by an old friend." Another pause, this time broken by Alexis. "We'd better go. Do you need to get anything from your car?"

"Just my briefcase." She fetched it and settled into the passenger seat next to Alexis.

Alexis edged out into the small network of the Ferndown Estate roads and turned onto the lane that would take them down to the main Portsmouth road.

"It's so handy for the college here, and such lovely views," Rosemary said, turning back to look at the neat new houses. "I'd like to find out a little more about the history of the place. Someone told me there was once a big house on the land."

No, thought Alexis, you would not want to know about the history of the place. You would not want to know about the big house, still less what happened there. She felt the old anger stir within her, and it felt good. She had judged this moment right, and it was time once more to avenge the wrong, time to do Her bidding once again. With her right hand, lightly and with practiced touch, she caressed the head of the golden snake necklace.

"I think there's some information about it in the History Centre," Rosemary continued. "Next time I'm in Woking I must pop in and see what they've got."

Alexis felt the snake release its jaws and quicken against her, its body tensing as it took control of its own weight and became again sinew, bone and venom. For a moment it paused, drawing strength and vigour from the warmth of Alexis's body, then began, almost imperceptibly, the circumnavigation of her neck towards its prey.

"I believe it was a Victorian mansion," said Alexis. "I saw a picture of it once." She was driving slowly, as the narrow lane required. Slowly enough too for the task in hand to be complete by the journey's end. Rosemary was oblivious to the stealthy progress of the snake behind her, across the gap between the two front seats.

"Is it OK if I drop you off at the main gate?" asked Alexis.

"Of course, I can easily walk down the drive. It's really very kind of you."

Rosemary Nugent never saw what it was that brushed briefly against her and struck once with deadly aim. She felt a sharp pain as the snake's jaws closed on the flesh of her neck, delivering its venom directly into the bloodstream. She put up her hand, but before it even reached the wound the neurotoxin was coursing through her body. She struggled to draw breath, her arms flailing uselessly as waves of panic and pain swept through her body. Her eyes lost focus and all power of speech deserted her, her screams dying on her lips as paralysis set in.

Alexis Tobin paused briefly in a layby lest her passenger's spasms interfere with her control of the car. When they had sufficiently abated, she drove on. Death, she knew, was by now inevitable and would come in as little as thirty minutes. She turned left onto the Portsmouth road. Rosemary's heart rate had fallen, and her blood pressure was by now dangerously low as the powerful poison took hold of her nervous system. Alexis glanced behind to check that her serpent was safe in the back of the car. She pulled in at the bus stop serving the main entrance to the college, and after unfastening Rosemary's seat belt, she got out of the car and walked round to open the front passenger door.

With some exertion Alexis transferred the near-lifeless Rosemary from the passenger seat to the wooden bench at the bus stop. Casual passers-by would not notice anything amiss – indeed it would be more than an hour before the body of the Law lecturer was discovered by a colleague and the alarm raised.

As she drove back up the steep escarpment of the foothills of the North Downs, Alexis felt the caress of the snake as it settled back into its familiar place around her neck. Its jaws locked onto the tail, the dull brown body turned to gold and the hooded head to turquoise. Raising her right hand, she traced the outline of the clasp and said quietly,

"It's what we're here for."

FEBRUARY 1871

"We shall make a fresh start in Plymouth, Henry dearest. Now we are free of this place, you will recover, and all shall be well again. Wait and see."

Sarah Maddox allowed herself a final look at Ferndown as their carriage wound its way down the long drive for the last time: the arched windows, the domed tower, the turrets and terrace, all made flat and grey by the thin February light.

"Let us hope you are right, my dear. It can scarce be worse than before."

She took his hand in hers, and their eyes met. "Whatever it was, it will not follow you. Of that I am certain."

Sarah Maddox now knew that somehow the villa itself was the cause of her husband's descent into a place of anguish that she could neither comprehend nor hope to ease as long as it was their home. As the carriage turned onto the Portsmouth road, she felt a weight lift from her and sensed that the ordeal of the last year was coming to an end.

Henry Maddox stared through the window of the brougham with a fixed, unseeing gaze. Their journey to the station would take him, for the first time since it all began, past the brewery where he had once held sway as Master Brewer. Even if he averted his eyes, he knew that as they approached, the bitter-sweet smell from the mash tuns would pervade the carriage, taunting his recent loss of status.

He turned to look at his wife, seated opposite him. At first he thought there must be some trick of the light, some reflection that caused his eyes to falter. But as the carriage moved from shade into light, there was no mistaking it. On the vacant seat next to her a human-like shape was materialising. At first indistinct and shadowy, it slowly thickened into solid form.

"No. No!" Henry Maddox could hardly speak for terror.

"Why Henry, whatever is it?"

Maddox raised his hand to point at the apparition.

"There! There! It is her! She is here!"

Sarah Maddox turned her head to look at the seat next to her. "Where, Henry? There is nothing there."

The apparition had by now acquired features and declared itself to be that of an old woman. Her head was bowed; her chin sunk into what appeared to Maddox to be folds of thick grey gauze. Unable to avert his eyes, he watched in horror as the spectre raised its head.

Sarah Maddox saw her husband's face drain white with dread. She could not begin to guess what horrors he was seeing; she could not see the gaunt, hideous face, the thin lips pulled into a ghastly smile, the eyes that seemed to penetrate his very being. She could not feel the hatred that now pervaded the cramped interior of the carriage; she could not hear the voice that Maddox knew from before, so close that the spectre needed barely to whisper the words:

"I bring you nightmares, torment and despair."

The last word was drawn out, as if the exhalation were the old crone's last breath. It was too much for Henry Maddox. His heart, weakened by months of affliction, leapt in his breast one last time, and he fell forwards with a choking cry. By the time his frame fell against the vacant seat opposite, he was already dead.

THE PRESENT

"Come and have a look at this, Caroline."

Paul Conrad's desk was covered with printouts: census returns, maps of different dates and scales, scanned pages of newspapers, telephone directories and trade catalogues. His wife surveyed the scene. "You've been busy."

"There's something really odd going on here. This house, Ferndown – the one near Weyford. Partridge builds it in 1870 for Henry Maddox, the brewer. Then there's half a dozen different owners up to about 1910, after which, zilch. No-one recorded as living there. No census records, no telephone numbers, nothing."

"So?"

"Just that it's on all the maps up until the early 1960s – look, here it is in 1923, still there in the mid-thirties, 1947, 1953," and he piled the copies of the maps one on top the other, "Until 1961, when it disappears. And of course it's not there now – the satellite pictures show a clearing, surrounded by this new estate built in the late 60s."

Since Paul's retirement, he and his wife had found a new interest in one of the less-travelled byways of architectural history. Paul's great-grandfather, Charles Partridge, had for a brief decade in mid-Victorian Britain created and then satisfied a market for building in concrete, long before it was either fashionable or avant-garde. At the time, his buildings were considered by many to be unconventional, and they had over the years either been knocked down because they were unconventional or stayed put because, being concrete, they were very difficult to knock down.

Ferndown seemed to be a mixture of both. Unconventional would hardly begin to describe the villa that had once graced the North Downs. Ornate, pilastered and turreted, it was a confection in concrete. Yet by Paul's reckoning it had stayed put long after anyone lived in it: only decades after it was last inhabited was it actually demolished.

Caroline looked at a print of the house from part of a double-page spread in an architectural magazine of the 1870s.

"What I don't get is why Maddox lived there for such a short time," continued Paul. "He spent all that money on it – I mean look at it, it's a stately home, practically – and barely a year later, he's gone. He doesn't even make it into the 1871 census. Come to think of it, nobody seems to have lived there very long, do they?"

"Perhaps we should go and take a look," said Caroline, "but I don't expect there's much to see now."

THE PAST

1870

THE CLIENTS

"Mr Westmacott, sir!"

William Westmacott, architect and surveyor, picked his way carefully through the undergrowth covering the site of his latest commission, towards the source of the greeting.

"Mr Maddox! And Mrs Maddox, too! You have secured a fine piece of land. Why, I would guess you can see as far as Richmond Hill."

"Five counties, Mr Westmacott, five counties. And thirty churches. Maybe more from the top of the tower, who knows?"

"The tower? I don't see one."

"The tower, Mr Westmacott, that you are about to design for us. Somewhere about here, I fancy." Henry Maddox strode to the edge of the escarpment where the land fell off steeply to the north. "And beyond that, we shall have a terrace, maybe. Or a par-terre, as I believe they call it in this part of the world." His northern accent split the word with studied deliberation.

"We shall ask you to pay particular attention to the grounds, Mr Westmacott." Sarah Maddox cast a knowledgeable eye over the site. "You are I expect familiar with my family's place, Bramford Park."

"Of course, Mrs Maddox – if I am not mistaken it is visible beyond the trees over there." Of course. There could be few people in the county who would not have heard of Bramford Park, a large estate to the south of Weyford. On rising ground in the centre of the park stood a fine Queen Anne house, built by Sarah Maddox's ancestors a century and a half previously on the proceeds of successful commerce in the East India Company. Surely, thought William Westmacott, he was not being asked to replicate such grandeur here, on this four-acre site?

"Then you will understand how a house must be at ease with itself in its grounds. The landscaping is everything. As Henry says, we shall have some formal terracing near the house, and as the land falls away the grounds will become wilder."

"We shall have a great hall, Mr Westmacott, and a grand staircase." Gesticulating in step with his thoughts, Henry Maddox paced across the rough grass as if it were already home to the imagined building. "And a large drawing room, a library and a billiard room."

"And leading from the drawing room we shall have a conservatory for my ferns. They are a particular favourite of mine." Sarah Maddox continued her husband's train of thought. "Upstairs we shall require at least eight bedrooms. We have five daughters, and then there will be the usual servants' rooms."

William Westmacott was keenly aware how much depended on the success of this project, for these were no ordinary clients. Since his appointment as Master Brewer at Priory Ales, Henry Maddox had become a well-known and well-liked figure in the Weyford community. The Surrey market town was a long way, both in distance and manner, from his native Yorkshire, but he was a practical man whose common sense and outgoing nature won him friends across the social spectrum. He was equally at ease discussing barley varieties with the landed gentry, the year's hop harvest with the agricultural workers, or the qualities of a good working horse with the ostlers at the Angel Hotel. Scarcely a soul in the town was untouched by his skills with malt and hop, and the name of Henry Maddox was honoured in the hostelries where his ales were sold.

Maddox had enhanced his status by marrying into the local gentry. Sarah brought with her an enviably wide social circle, and her knowledge and skill as an amateur horticulturalist made her, in her husband's eyes, much to be preferred over the generality of her peers. She understood her husband's passion for his craft, and he took delight in her knowledge of plants, in particular of the ferns that she had made her speciality.

So far, inspiration had not struck William Westmacott. The more he came to know his clients, the more he realised that this would be no conventional house. Those he had designed by the score; some had even been written up and illustrated in the pages of *The Building News*: 'A Large Country Rectory;' 'A Villa for a Sculptor;' 'A Double Suburban Villa.' But, 'A Villa for Henry Maddox, Master Brewer' – and indeed for the Master Brewer's wife – the concept had eluded him. But by meeting his clients at the new villa's location, a site high in the North Downs, he began to understand better the workings of their minds, and how he might satisfy their requirements. That just left the issue of cost. The budget was tight, and his clients' expectations exceeded their means. That was a problem for which, as yet, he had no solution. His deliberations were interrupted by Henry Maddox.

"And we shall have the very latest ideas throughout. Take concrete. Are you aware of Mr Partridge? He is a pioneer in the use of concrete, and a first-rate builder. He has done me proud with the new beer store at the brewery. All in concrete, made with Portland cement, of course. The finest vaulting you can imagine, and half the price of brick. All the heating and ventilation is carried through the building in channels in the walls – just like the Romans did, but with modern materials. Have you ever built in concrete, Mr Westmacott?"

William Westmacott struggled to keep up with his client's train of thought. "Er, not yet, Mr Maddox, though I have heard there is much merit in it."

"Indeed, it is the coming thing, I can assure you. You must come and see for yourself."

"Thank you, I should be delighted to do so."

"We shall look forward to seeing your plans, Mr Westmacott," said Sarah Maddox. "Our villa will be the talk of the town, I do declare. Come, Henry." The couple made their way to their waiting carriage.

William Westmacott returned to his office in Mill Street. There he pinned a sheet of paper to his drawing board and for several hours his hands moved swiftly across the smooth surface. It would be a gamble, he knew, but at last he could see a way to meet the Maddox's extravagant requirements at a price they could afford. He worked long into the evening, his ideas beginning to take shape.

Henry Maddox was as good as his word. At his invitation, a few days later William Westmacott was making his way back down towards the river for a conducted tour, by its Master Brewer, of the Priory Brewery. Few could be unaware of its presence, for a rich tangy aroma from the brewing process pervaded the town in due season, carrying with it the promise of good cheer to come. In Weyford, Priory Ales oiled the wheels of business from the cattle market to the Corn Exchange.

They toasted harvest home at the Jolly Farmer, rang in the New Year at the Bell, and made tall the hunters' tales at the Fox and Hounds.

The brewery itself was less noticed since it occupied a riverside site at the lowest point of the town; and its chimneys, towers and brew houses, when viewed from the surrounding hills, neither stood out on any horizon nor stopped the eye with any single well-defined building. Instead the brewery presented a bewildering conglomeration of buildings of different shapes, sizes and styles, reflecting partly the different trades and functions which they housed, and partly their gradual accretion as the business had expanded over the years. The latest, and the focus of William Westmacott's visit, was a large four-storey building with a steeply pitched roof, its walls punctuated regularly with arched windows. Unlike its brick neighbours, it was rendered in a cement stucco, lined out to imitate stone.

Any sense of confusion externally was dispelled as soon as William Westmacott entered the brewery with his host. "Now, Mr Westmacott, you shall see how the process works, from start to finish." The two men had climbed to the top of the building housing the mash tuns. They entered a room which covered the entire area of the building, strewn with barley. Four men, whose task it was to turn the grain with large shovels, stopped work briefly as Maddox greeted them and introduced his visitor. "This is where we store the malt before it is ground up – and that happens on the floor below us. Every day we can crush enough to brew twelve thousand gallons." Westmacott was almost overcome by the intense aromas and the noise of the grinding machines below their feet. "We use a steam engine to power all this," he heard Maddox say over the din.

The tour followed the progress of the malt through the brewing process, as it fell through chutes and was carried along by giant Archimedes screws into revolving cylinders. All the while Henry Maddox described and explained. "And now the grist and the liquor can be mixed in the mash tuns – we have two of them here," he said. "When that's done, we let it all stand; then we sparge it – that's what those sprayers are – and it's ready for boiling with the hops. We shall go next door to see that." The Master Brewer set off at a rate which left Westmacott struggling to keep pace.

The giant coppers for boiling the wort were housed in their own building. "Two and a half thousand gallons in each, Mr Westmacott, and heated by gas – the very latest thing. And all the water comes from a tank in that tower – it's a large as a swimming bath." Westmacott looked mesmerised as the liquor was poured into the coppers, then watched it seething and boiling, the surface flecked with foam. He felt himself becoming intoxicated, and it came as a relief to climb up to the well-ventilated fermentation area where a series of large shallow tanks cooled the wort before it flowed down into the fermentation tuns. "So you see, Mr Westmacott, it's all done with gravity – from here it flows down into the conditioning tanks, and then it's ready for the cask."

The heady smell of the now finished beer hit them as they entered the racking room, where a constant supply of oak casks, carried on a series of chain conveyors, were filled by a workforce of dozens of men and rolled back heavily onto the conveyors. "And from here, the casks go to the beer store, which is why you came here in the first place, is it not?" Maddox paused to discuss a technical matter with the foreman of the room, then escorted Westmacott towards their final destination. "You will, I think, find it most interesting."

Westmacott drew his breath sharply at the size and scale of the building. Above them, a vaulted roof four bays wide extended into the middle distance, each vault intersecting with its neighbour in an intricate and harmonious pattern not unlike a cathedral, save that they sprang from a grid of slender cast iron columns. The floor area was filled with rack upon rack of beer casks, raised on wooden trestles. "We have four floors, each built in the same manner – all in cast concrete," said Henry Maddox, "This man Partridge I was telling you about – he has a set of patent machines for concrete building. It all went up very quickly – two feet a day, I believe."

Westmacott walked over to one of the walls and inspected it. The interior of the building appeared unfinished, the walls remaining as they had emerged from the shuttering in which the concrete was cast. "Most intriguing. And cheaper than brick, you say?"

"Half the price, and I dare say twice as strong, when you look at how it's built. The vaulting can bear many tons, as you can see. And the heating and ventilation is all carried in channels in the walls – we need to maintain a constant sixty degrees, summer and winter."

Despite the crude interior finish and its industrial purpose, the building was lofty, spacious and elegant. Like all he had seen on his visit, it impressed the architect and set many thoughts racing in his mind. The brewery, he now realised, far from being an incoherent jumble of giant sheds, was more like a vast machine: the buildings' shapes and sizes were determined by the array of vats, tuns, cylinders, tanks, hoppers, pipes and barrels which they supported and protected. But above all, he had learned more about the man who managed and made sense of the whole.   After enjoying a glass of the brewery's finest India Pale Ale, he thanked his host, "You have given me much to think about, Mr Maddox."

"When shall we see your first designs for the villa, Mr Westmacott? Shall we say in a week's time?"

"A week will be enough. I shall look forward to it. Good day, Mr Maddox."

"And good day to you, Mr Westmacott."

The architect walked to the gate, turned to take one last look at the brewery complex, and strode up the High Street with renewed purpose.

For the next four days William Westmacott worked almost without a break. His first task was to take, with his assistant, detailed measurements of the site. Where the land fell away to the north, he made accurate measurements of the slope; where it was level, he plotted where the villa would stand to best advantage. Once he had determined its position, he sketched in the landscaping that was so important to Sarah Maddox: the terrace, the lawns, the borders, the kitchen garden, all these fell naturally into place. In the centre, dominating the site, and no doubt visible for miles around, was the villa. At first a series of rough sketches in his notebook, it gradually took shape and form, reflecting the diversity of functions which his clients had specified. Only when he was satisfied with the harmony of the whole, did he start on the detailed drawings that he would present to them the following week.

The fifth day saw Westmacott absent from his office and from the town. It was a day, he knew, that would be pivotal in his career, and the meeting he had arranged in

London would determine its course. The train journey allowed him space to clarify his thoughts. He stared with unseeing eyes at the passing Surrey landscape as he rehearsed the arguments for and against the idea he had formulated on site and tested at the brewery. *For:* his clients, in their different ways, were both influential people; there was the prospect that their satisfaction would bring new clients to his door. *Against:* his rivals would take every opportunity to dismiss the villa as a sham, a fraud, and an affront to polite architecture, and this could result in his losing new business. *For:* he would become a pioneer in the latest techniques and materials, with all the rewards that such a daring approach could bring. *Against:* he had never before attempted such a novel method of construction, and the personal and professional risk was considerable.

Another consideration was his recent application for fellowship of the RIBA: that too could turn on the success or failure of this project. It would not be an easy decision. He read for the hundredth time the advertisement in *The Building News* that had prompted the day's meeting, with its list of satisfied clients and unsolicited testimonials. He folded the magazine into his briefcase. His train had arrived at Waterloo.

—◈◈◈—

Mill Street was a short spur off the High Street, flanked by houses with elegant Georgian facades behind which Weyford's professional classes carried on their occupations. Number Twelve had a yellow front door on which a number of brass plates advertised the presence of two solicitors, an actuary and, on the top floor, "William Westmacott, Architect and Surveyor". It was to this set of rooms that, three days later, the architect welcomed his clients. The stairs became narrower and steeper as the storeys rose, but the visitors were rewarded with a view that took in the meandering curve of the river and the locks of its navigable canal, and beyond, the ruins of the castle. William Westmacott ushered his clients to a large mahogany table on which lay a number of rolled-up drawings.

"I have, I hope, understood your instructions correctly, and I trust you will be pleased with my designs." He reached for one of the sheets and slowly rolled it out across the table, revealing a perspective drawing of the villa, favouring the front and left side.

"Why Mr Westmacott, it is magnificent," said Sarah Maddox.

"Ay, that it is," echoed her husband, his voice quiet, as if taken by surprise. "A grand place indeed."

The drawings showed a four-square Italianate building, fronted by a retaining wall with steps leading to the grounds below. The walls were punctuated with tall pilasters rising the entire two-storey height of the villa and topped with a pediment behind which rose a tiled roof. The windows were either squared-off or had semi-circular arches, all with elaborate mouldings above and below. The frontage was dominated by a tall tower taken to a height of three storeys, the uppermost room surmounted by a dome with an ornate pinnacle.

"Allow me to explain it to you," said William Westmacott. "I have attempted to marry antiquity with modernity, taking the best from each age. The plan, which you will see here," and he unrolled another sheet, "the plan is inspired by classical Rome. The villa is built around a central hall, or atrium, in the same way as the Romans built theirs. The atrium extends the full height of the villa, and I have added a glass roof that will provide light to the central core and shelter from the elements. The principal rooms depend off it at both the ground and the first floor. So here we see the dining room, the library, and the billiard room, and on this side the drawing room with morning room adjoining to one side, and the conservatory to the other. The drawing room has French windows leading to the garden, and the conservatory has similar access to the grounds. The first floor rooms are reached by a grand double staircase, and I propose to install a large mirror at the half landing, to reflect the room on itself. The gallery extends around the atrium on three sides at first-floor level."

The villa was indeed on the grand scale, and Henry Maddox appeared momentarily and, unusually, lost for words. He stared at the perspective drawing, his hand moving across it as if to aid his comprehension. "You have given us our tower, too, I see."

"The tower provides the entrance vestibule to the villa at ground level; above there is a bedroom, with a staircase leading to a turret which has clear views in all directions. It is surmounted by this cupola, with finials at each corner."

"Why, it is just as I would have hoped for, Mr Westmacott, and much more besides. How many rooms are there?"

"Twenty-two in all, Mr Maddox, including the basement rooms."

"Twenty-two rooms. That should be enough for us and the girls, don't you agree, my dear?"

"It is most handsome. This 'atrium' of yours will be a splendid place for entertaining. Now, the terrace, Mr Westmacott, you have indicated some planting on it, and beyond."

"Indeed, Mrs Maddox, I propose some formal planting close to the house and larger plantations with shrubs beyond. But you will have your own ideas of these – I merely make suggestions."

"If it is modelled on a Roman villa, there must be topiary. The Romans were most skilled in shaping box and yew. I shall have to consult the classical works in the library at Bramford."

"I can see all the antiquity, Mr Westmacott," said Henry Maddox, "But where's the modernity?"

"The villa will incorporate the most advanced ideas. For heating and ventilation, channels in the walls will carry warm air in winter and cool air in summer. The house will be heated by a single stove, here in the basement, with heat exchangers to allow the air to be warmed and conducted away. Each room will be equipped with vents which allow a comfortable temperature to be maintained at all times. We shall specify the latest electric bells, of Mr Moseley's patent, and the water closets will all be of the latest pattern."

"Channels in the walls, you say, Mr Westmacott? Your stonework here will not admit readily to having channels cut in it, surely?"

Westmacott drew breath. It was time to cast the die.

"Mr Maddox, I am going to propose that we build the entire villa in concrete. I have seen your new building at the brewery, and I have also this week had detailed discussions with your Mr Partridge, the concrete patentee, who assures me that there are no obstacles to such an approach, even for a grand villa. Indeed, I am convinced that there are many advantages to be had."

His proposal was met with a prolonged silence. Then Henry Maddox spoke.

"Concrete, eh, Mr Westmacott? Concrete. A villa in concrete. A Roman villa. In modern concrete." William Westmacott was unsure from Maddox's musings whether his idea had met with favour. Then, to the architect's relief, his client broke into a broad smile.

"Why, Mr Westmacott, I can see you are a man after my own heart. And you have even used my ideas for the heating and ventilation!" For the first time since he arrived, Maddox appeared at ease, both with himself and with his architect. "I think it is a splendid idea! What do you think, Sarah, my dear?"

"I hardly know what to think. Of course, Henry, I can see that concrete is used to great effect in your beer store, and my father's clerk of works recently built some farm labourers' cottages on the estate in the same material. But a villa on this scale! How will you achieve all this ornamentation in concrete, Mr Westmacott?"

"With respect, madam, it is no different than if the walls were made of brick. The villa has a rendering of cement to cover the roughness of the concrete as it emerges from the mould, and this can be treated in the same way as any stucco finish. Mr Partridge says that this is the natural finish for a concrete structure. Furthermore, he argues that if the building is to have a stucco exterior, there is little merit in building expensively in brick, which will all be covered over. He assures me that concrete is both stronger and cheaper than either brick or stone."

"Mr Westmacott, when we built the beer store, Mr Partridge encouraged me to employ my brewery labourers to mix and pour the concrete. The men were pleased to receive additional money out of season, and their wages were less than those of bricklayers and stone-masons. Could we adopt such a method here?" Henry Maddox waved his hand over the plans.

"I have no doubt that Mr Partridge would be amenable to such a suggestion. He gave me a prospectus for his firm which lists all the benefits of his apparatus, and the use of unskilled labour is certainly one of them. Maybe if I left it with you for a few days, you could consider the proposal at your leisure?"

"Can you give us some idea as to the cost of this approach as against a more conventional construction, Mr Westmacott?" asked Sarah Maddox.

"Mr Partridge puts the cost of raising the walls at half that of brick or stone, but to that one must add the cost of finishing the building and, of course, all other costs remain the same. I estimate that the villa with the stables and coachhouse together would cost four thousand pounds in concrete, against six thousand in brick."

"Well, Mr Westmacott, you have now given us much to think about. We must thank you for your ingenious solution. We will take these plans and study them, and we shall give you our response within the week."

Henry Maddox bundled the plans together into a roll, which Westmacott tied with a length of red tape.

"I shall look forward to learning of your decision," Westmacott replied, as he showed his clients out. The Master Brewer and his wife descended the twisting staircase and stepped into the street.

The more Henry Maddox looked at the plans, the more his enthusiasm grew for the architect's concept. He looked over them one more time before retiring, noting the grandeur of the atrium with its staircase and gallery, the vaulting in the basement and the combined heating and ventilation ducts. "A Roman villa, but for our time. He's done us proud, he has," he said to himself. But his sleep was restless: he had been unable to gauge his wife's response to Westmacott's proposal to build in concrete, and he had held back from asking her directly. He was nervous that, sensing his enthusiasm, she might agree to its use against her better judgment. After twenty years of marriage he knew to trust her instinct, and on a matter as important as this nothing but her wholehearted support would do.

A few days later, it was Sarah Maddox who absented herself from the market town. Her mission was not dissimilar to William Westmacott's the week before, though her journey was shorter than his, and more familiar. Benjamin Webster, clerk of works to Viscount Melhuish, was surprised to see her carriage draw up outside his office at Bramford Park, and still more so when Sarah Maddox announced the reason for her visit to her family's estate.

That evening Henry Maddox resolved to broach the subject of the villa with his wife.

"Have you had a chance to consider Mr Westmacott's proposals, my dear?" he asked. "I shall be most interested to hear your thoughts."

"Indeed I have, Henry. Mr Westmacott's design is nothing short of a *tour de force*. It has much to recommend it."

"And are you in favour of his choice of material for its construction?"

"I have spent the day in the company of Mr Webster, my father's clerk of works. He speaks highly of the use of concrete and has recently employed it on the estate, though of course it has not been used in a villa on this scale before. He tells me the Duke of Caithness has taken it up on his land in Scotland too."

"And does that persuade you that it would be appropriate here?" asked Maddox.

"Not at all. The circumstances north of the border are quite different to ours here in Surrey, so the two are not comparable."

Henry Maddox's heart sank. So she was un-convinced. He would not try to persuade her.

"No, there are many reasons closer to home why, in my opinion, we should use it in the construction of the villa."

Why we should use it? Had he misheard?

"Mr Webster is a leading light in the Society for Improving the Condition of the Labouring Classes, a cause which, as you know, I too hold dear. We visited one of his new concrete cottages today, and I was able to speak with Daniel Fowler, who has worked on the Bramford estate for twenty years. He cannot speak highly enough of his new accommodation, and his wife told me it is the first house she has ever lived in that is free from damp and vermin."

"I am pleased to hear it, my dear, but I fail to see why you think that is a reason for us to adopt it. We are hardly likely to suffer from either, whatever material we choose."

"Mr Webster tells me that there are many landowners who speak out against the use of concrete as a building material. They say that it shrinks and cracks, which he insists is not true."

"Ay, Mr Partridge assures us on that point also in his prospectus." Maddox was still unsure where his wife's reasoning was taking them. Sarah Maddox continued.

"And they use that as an excuse not to build decent houses for their labourers. Mr Webster's cottages cost only a hundred and seventy pounds each to build. At that price he can let them out at a rent that the labourers can afford. While on other estates they are forced to live in houses that we would not consider fit for animals."

"And that is why we should build in concrete too?"

"Of course it is." Sarah Maddox's frustration was evident in her tone and her complexion. "We need to set an example, Henry. If we show that concrete is a suitable material for a grand house, maybe it will become more generally used. How else are we to improve the living conditions of the labouring classes?"

"Since you put it like that, my dear, I am happy to agree with you. So, we should tell Mr Westmacott to proceed with the plans as he has specified?"

"We most certainly should. Henry, dearest, we shall be pioneers."

William Westmacott received the news with some trepidation. The whole project now seemed laden with risk. This would be his first experiment in the use of concrete, and he was nervous at how much faith he would have to place in the contractor, Charles Partridge. There would be none of the traditional skills of bricklaying or stonemasonry on this site, and the mixing and pouring of the concrete would be carried out by men who were hired simply for their physical strength. Had anything on a similar scale been attempted, he wondered. Then he recalled the wording of the advertisement: 'Suitable for any class or size of building,' and he said quietly to himself,

"I do hope so, I do hope so."

'A Roman Villa, but for Our Time'

Charles Partridge, builder in concrete, climbed the steps of the terrace two at a time. "We are ahead of schedule, Mr Westmacott. We have already made a start on the walls." The two men stood for a while atop a long concrete retaining wall, behind which the ground had been levelled to make a platform for the villa. The length of the wall was punctuated by sloping pilasters, and a central set of steps led to the lower ground where it fell away to the north.

"Very good, Mr Partridge, you are as good as your word. This is indeed a most interesting project. I must say, however, that until I saw your beer store at the brewery, I was of the opinion that concrete is better suited to simpler dwellings – cottages for agricultural workers perhaps, or even farm buildings."

Charles Partridge fixed his gaze on the architect. "Mr Westmacott, nothing will give me greater pleasure than to demonstrate to you what this material is capable of. You shall see."

The site was hardly recognisable from Westmacott's first visit. The dense vegetation had been cleared, and the ground laid bare. The outline of the walls was visible in the earth where the foundations had been dug, and a team of men was at work setting the long iron troughs that would contain the concrete until it was set hard. Where these had already been installed, another group was tipping barrowfuls of wet concrete between the parallel panels. "Five weeks, no more, and then we shall hand it over for finishing," said Charles Partridge. "But we shall need all the men Mr Maddox can spare."

"It is certainly a most singular method of construction. To use unskilled labour, and such an unconventional technique; it is all very novel."

"Unconventional maybe, Mr Westmacott, but as to novel, there I cannot agree. Why, as you are well aware, the Romans were expert at building in concrete. And an apt comparison, if I may say so, given your design."

Charles Partridge broke off and crossed to where two large machines had been installed. One had a pair of iron rollers mounted beneath a hopper; the other a horizontal drum with rotating beaters inside. Both were driven by belts from a contractor's engine, a wheeled steam boiler with valves, pistons and flywheels on a horizontal cylinder. Nearby was a large mound of broken bricks and stone. "Is there any more of this on the site, Joseph?" he asked of one of his men. "Maybe a little, Mr Partridge, sir, but we have scoured the area as you told us." "Very good. Make sure it is thoroughly washed and crushed, and only then should you cast it into the mixer. And remember, seven parts aggregate to one of cement."

"Yes, Mr Partridge."

"So there you see, Mr Westmacott, how we can make savings. Half the cost of brick or stone, if we can use what we find on site. We are fortunate here – there is plenty of stone, and some old bricks and tile beside, which we can break up. My patent stone crusher reduces everything to the same size. It all helps."

William Westmacott found it difficult to hear above the noise of the machinery. This was unlike any building site he had ever visited. The stone crusher gave out a series of ear-splitting cracks, groans and roars as its pair of studded rollers slowly ground the rubble into fragments. These rattled down a chute and were funnelled into a waiting barrow. Two men kept the hopper fed constantly with new material, while two more ensured that there was always a barrow in place to catch the falling pellets. These were in turn unloaded into the waiting mouth of the second machine, mixed with cement and water, and churned in its large rotating iron drum. The resulting concrete was disgorged and wheeled to the rectangular grid of iron troughs that formed the mould for the walls of the house. There was no let-up in this ceaseless round of supply and demand.

The din of the grinding and mixing machines was augmented by the rhythmic thumping and hissing of the stationary steam engine. It was operated by a tall man dressed all in black, whose sole task was to ensure that the engine never faltered in its propulsion of the machines. The long leather belts connecting them whipped and slapped as they whirled around wide pulley-wheels. The heat and smoke from the boiler's chimney drifted across the building site, mingling with the smell of steam and hot oil.

"It is indeed remarkable, Mr Partridge. And you say you can raise the walls by two feet a day?" William Westmacott had to shout to make himself heard.

"Two feet, every day," came the reply. "We reset the ironwork on top of the previous day's work and fill it up again. When all's done, we put a skim of cement over the whole wall and mark it out with lines to imitate stone."

Westmacott looked at the apparatus arrayed on the site and at the incessant efforts of the labourers to satisfy its demands. "I fear for these poor men, Mr Partridge. They appear to be driven by the machines. One might have hoped things to be the other way around."

"We must make the most of the engine while we have it on site, Mr Westmacott. Every minute it stands idle is time, and money, wasted."

"Very well, but for me it still feels like a step into the unknown. I am used to seeing bricklayers and stone-masons at work on my buildings. Most of the people I see here are borrowed from Mr Maddox's brewery. They have none of the skills of the builder."

"There are skills a-plenty here," said Charles Partridge. "Take my men over there," and he gestured to the team setting in place the concrete-building apparatus. "A single error in positioning the frame will result in a wall being out of true. If it is not vertical, the wall will lean; if it is not level, the wall will slope. Where they meet, the angle must be exactly square. In that respect it is no different from brick. And I think we are agreed on another point: if you are intending to finish the walls in stucco, why go to the expense of building in brick? Concrete is stronger by far, and once it is covered, you will never discern what is underneath."

"I shall look forward to seeing the finished work, Mr Partridge. I can see that you supply, in the words of the great Vitruvius, both commodity and firmness. Now I shall have to see how we can add his third ingredient of great architecture, delight."

"Ay, well, with me, Mr Westmacott, handsome is as handsome does. And that for me is the great beauty of concrete."

"Indeed, Mr Partridge, I think we speak the same language."

Charles Partridge looked quizzically at William Westmacott. He was not entirely convinced of this last assertion, but he let it pass.

—❧—

A visitor to Ferndown six months after its completion could have been forgiven for imagining the villa to have stood for as many years. What until recently had been bare earth was now a garden of mature trees and shrubs, and borders filled with gaily coloured flowers. The four-acre site had been subdivided into a series of individual gardens, each dedicated to different species and styles of planting, and each leading naturally from one to the other with carefully contrived paths and features to entice the eye. Nearer the villa, the planting became more formal with geometrically laid out beds and topiary work, of box, yew and cypress sculpted into animals, birds, and the solid geometry of spheres, pyramids and spirals. The villa was approached from the gardens up twin staircases built out from the sloping retaining wall of the terrace, along which were a series of urns spilling greenery and colour.

The house was similarly fitted out, its bare concrete walls now plastered and papered, and the rooms furnished in the latest fashion. Sarah Maddox's skill as a garden designer was more than matched by her flair for interiors: every day had seen a succession of horse-drawn delivery vans bringing carpets, curtains and furniture, the empty shell of the house gradually being transformed into a luxurious home.

There had been such interest in the design of the villa and its unorthodox method of construction that

Henry Maddox proposed throwing the place open to the press and other interested visitors. And so it was that one day in June a steady stream of carriages bearing inquisitive visitors from town and county converged on the newly completed mansion. The day had dawned fair and bright, the light so clear that from the high vantage point of the new villa it seemed possible almost to reach out and touch the distant hills.

"As soon as Mr Westmacott showed us his drawings, I knew it would be delightful," Sarah Maddox led the writer from *The Building News* by the arm along the terrace towards the main entrance. "'A Roman villa, but for our time,' is what he promised us. You will find it has every modern comfort you could ask for, with all the grandeur of the Roman style." They walked up the steps to the entrance hall, above which rose the tall tower topped with a dome. As they entered the great hall, Edward Wilson stopped and stared.

"Why it is quite splendid, Mrs Maddox. I have seldom seen such a spectacle."

"Mr Westmacott says we must call it the atrium. It is the name the Romans gave to a courtyard – but cleverly he has added a roof to keep us dry. Our climate is so very different from that of Italy."

It was indeed splendid. The large court rose the entire height of the house. Opposite the door was a grand double staircase with carved oak pilasters and handrails, leading to a broad gallery running round three sides. Behind the staircase was a vast mirror which gave the effect of doubling the size of the space. The room was covered by a clear glass roof, from the centre of which hung a large lantern with coloured glass inlays, and in its frame a motif of gilt ferns.

By now a number of people were beginning to fill the house, and the sounds of their wonder and surprise echoed in the great space.

"Twenty-two rooms including the basement . ."

"And have you seen the view from the tower?"

". . . as far as Richmond Hill . . ."

"The heating is most unusual – all done by ducts, apparently . . ."

". . . electric bells, you push the button. . ."

". . . and the whole building is in concrete. Imagine! No stone at all."

Henry Maddox led a small group of visitors through the conservatory and into the garden. "Outside we have over four acres; the shrubs and flowers are Mrs Maddox's favourites. And I challenge all comers to a game of croquet."

Sarah Maddox continued her tour with what had now grown to be a small group of journalists. "So you see, all the principal rooms open out from the atrium. The morning room gives on to the drawing room, and beyond that the conservatory, and on the other side of the house we have the dining room and the library, and the billiard room to the rear." Their tour brought them back into the great open space that formed the centre of the house.

"Mr Westmacott, how do you view your first experiment in concrete?" The journalist and architect stood together at the foot of the great staircase.

"I consider it most successful, Mr Wilson. It is proof that concrete can be used for any class or size of building."

"Ah, I perceive you have borrowed from the great Vitruvius," Edward Wilson pointed to three Latin words carved into the entablature of the gallery, one on each of its three sides, in large capital letters. "UTILITAS, FIRMITAS, VENUSTAS: commodity, firmness and delight. You would seem here to have achieved all three, if I may say so."

"And you see here, Mr Wilson, the figure of Venus herself, the very embodiment of delight." Henry Maddox's voice could be heard across the whole atrium. He was standing next to a large statue of a nearly naked female form, clutching in her left hand a drape around her hips, and holding it aloft with the other. A diving dolphin to one side complemented the curvaceous figure. The goddess cast her eyes down, her plaited hair tumbling over her left shoulder. Raised high on a plinth, the statue stood above all in the room and now formed the focus of their interest.

"Indeed, Mr Maddox, a most striking adornment."

"It is the creation of Mr Diamond, the architectural sculptor. He is an associate of Mr Partridge, who laid in place all the concrete."

"And is the statue also of concrete, Mr Maddox?" This from Sir Walter Turner, an eminent architect known for his love of natural materials and medieval crafts.

"It is I believe of marble fragments, Sir Walter, but cast in a similar way and polished."

"How very remarkable. Thank you, Mr Maddox."

Maddox appeared momentarily discomfited, but he pressed on. "Ladies and Gentlemen, I thank you all for coming today, and I trust you will have seen for yourselves how the latest ideas can be married to designs from antiquity. Mr Westmacott and I will be happy to answer any further questions, and then Mrs Maddox and I will invite you to partake of luncheon on the lawn. With, of course, as much Priory Ale as you may wish, to drink."

The group needed little further bidding, and soon some one hundred people were enjoying an al fresco meal in the grounds of the new villa. The Maddox's five daughters were drafted in to help the maid serve the guests, supervised by the cook, Mrs Hedges.

"You have done us proud, Mrs Hedges," Sarah Maddox said.

"Why, thank you, My Lady. It is a pleasure to work in such a well-appointed kitchen."

She then turned to the maid, "And Fanny, you too have excelled yourself. Our guests have expressed their thanks to me, but I know it is you and Mrs Hedges who deserve them the most."

They were joined by Henry Maddox. "Sarah, my dear, what a splendid idea to introduce a peacock to the terrace. It is a most appropriate addition."

"A peacock, dearest? I have not seen one. And I certainly did not make arrangements for such a bird."

Henry Maddox looked taken aback. "But I saw it with my own eyes. And you must surely have heard it?"

"Not once, my dear. Fanny, did you see a peacock on the terrace?"

"No, My Lady. Maybe it flew in from a neighbouring estate."

"I dare say that is the explanation. If it is still here later, Henry, we must call on our neighbours to arrange for its collection."

As the last of the day's visitors departed, Henry and Sarah Maddox stood together on the terrace. The afternoon sun slanted across the lawn, highlighting the detail of the pilasters on the face of the villa. "And now we have the place back to ourselves, Henry. I was correct to say it would be the talk of the town: I would go further and say it will be discussed across the county. Henry?" Sarah Maddox sensed that her husband was once more distracted.

"We still have one guest who has yet to take her leave of us," he said. "Fanny! Fanny!" The maid came running.

"Yes, Mr Maddox, sir,"

"Who is that lady who has just entered the vestibule? Dressed in a blue gown. Was she here earlier? I do not recall seeing her before."

"Sir, I haven't seen such a lady, and I have just come from there."

"Nonsense girl, why I can see her now quite clearly in the morning room."

"Sir, I see no-one."

"Then I shall have to go and look for myself. Come, my dear, and we shall make ourselves known to her." Henry Maddox almost dragged his wife towards the entrance hall and up the steps into the house. Once inside he took a sharp turning right and made straight for the morning room, whose windows gave onto the terrace. Sarah was almost running to keep up with him.

"Henry, dear, there is nobody in here. See."

Fanny ran weeping into the pantry. Mrs Hedges caught her in her arms. "Why Fanny, what is the matter?"

"The Master, Mrs Hedges. He has as good as accused me of neglecting one of our guests. But there is no-one in the morning room." Her tears were as much of fear as of sorrow. "And Mrs Maddox also said there is no-one there."

"Well, I don't know," said Mrs Hedges. "First a peacock, and now a phantom guest. If I didn't know the Master better, I would say he has taken too much Priory Ale."

THE HOUSE OF DREAMS

Henry Maddox's discomfort caused by the mysterious episode of the Lady in Blue was quietly put aside by his family and staff, but it continued to trouble him in the weeks that followed the Open Day. The brewery occupied most of his waking hours, and as July turned to August the preparations for brewing that season's bitter beer filled his working day. He found himself leaving earlier each morning and arriving home later. The pressures of work alone would be enough to justify this, but he experienced a curious feeling of relief on leaving the house, and a growing sense of foreboding as he arrived home at the end of the day. He had yet to admit it to himself, but Maddox did not feel at home in his new house. It would be hard to find a reason, for the architect had interpreted his requirements to the letter, indeed had exceeded his expectations; Sarah had wrought wonders in house and garden, and both she and their daughters professed themselves delighted with their new home. Henry Maddox was unable to share their contentment.

He found it difficult to settle in any of the principal rooms and took to wandering among them distractedly. In each room he sensed unseen eyes watching him, hostile and resentful of his intrusion. When he entered, he felt as if a conversation was suddenly silenced, himself its topic, and its tone malign and unwelcoming. Certain parts of the house he avoided visiting unless strictly necessary: the basement held a particular dread for him with its vaulted undercroft and the servants' offices at the foot of the stairs. It had a cold, claustrophobic atmosphere that he shunned.

It was the nights that he came to fear most. In the still of the midnight hour the small sounds of the house, the ticking of the clock, the rushing of the wind in the chimney, the hisses and pops of the gas mantle and the rattle of the sashes in their frames, these all seemed to coalesce into half-formed words close enough to resemble speech, too distant to interpret. The silence in the bedroom was broken by small echoing sounds coming from the ventilation grille as the stove cooled, the air in the duct whistling and wheezing as it adjusted to new temperatures. And from above came the soft hiss and drip of water as it replenished the supply in the tank. Sleep did not come easily to Maddox, and in the half-world between waking and sleeping he heard all these sounds as voices, muted, whispering, threatening. In his dreams the voices acquired more definition.

One, which became a recurrent nightmare, finds him alone in the drawing room of the house at nightfall, the setting sun casting long shadows through the west window and into the atrium. The room is full of voices scolding and cursing him, repeating the same words over and over in a tongue he does not understand: "*monstrum noctivagum ferimus,*" and then, "*diros cruciatus,*" overlapping and reinforcing each other in a tuneless fugue. He walks into the atrium where the voices change into a soft, menacing female chorus, half sung, with a falling, sighing cadence at the end of each phrase, "*nemo manere potest, non ullus tunc erit heres,*" again the words twisting and turning on themselves, wreathing and intertwining. Unwillingly and with growing terror, he finds himself descending to the basement, the stairway chill and unlit. In the housekeeper's room sits an old lady, her face at first masked by a cowl. She raises her head and turns to him, easing the cowl off her head to reveal not hair but a mass of snakes coiling around her face. Their heads turn towards him, their forked tongues darting. The old woman smiles, but her underlying expression is one of deep anger which he knows is unremitting and unrelenting. She addresses him in words he understands only too well:

"I bring you nightmares, torment and despair!
Here is no abiding stay. None shall here inherit!"

At this point he wakes, starting upright in bed with a cry which in his sleep-paralysed state he is barely able to articulate, "No!"

Sarah Maddox became increasingly concerned at her husband's changed behaviour. He himself could offer no explanation, and when challenged he retreated into denial. She confided in her closest confidante, her sister, but neither could suggest a satisfactory interpretation of his moods, nor find a solution. His distress continued through the last summer months with Maddox becoming increasingly ill at ease, his face drawn, and his jovial demeanour deserting him. One night towards the end of August he was troubled in his sleep by another recurring dream, this time with a fearful manifestation of the Lady in Blue.

In this dream he is in the garden among the newly planted topiary of birds and animals. It is a warm late summer day, the garden aloud with bees and heavy with heat. As he walks among the formal paths lined with box, one of the carefully clipped birds comes to life, springing off its evergreen perch and landing in front of him. It is a peacock. It stands facing him, its train fanned, threatening him and blocking his way. He turns to see behind him the figure of the Lady in Blue at the far end of the path. She is not close enough for him to read her expression, but he knows that she is fired with rage and that he is the object of her displeasure. The afternoon changes abruptly as the sky darkens, and he hears a distant rumble of thunder.

Maddox woke drenched in sweat. The knowledge that he had awoken from a dream brought no relief. It was time to face another day.

❧

One afternoon in early October Sarah Maddox was surprised to see a carriage drawing up to the house and her husband being helped out of it by two of his colleagues from the brewery, and a third person whom she identified as Doctor Voller, the family's physician. He drew her aside as Maddox was ushered into the drawing room.

"I must advise that your husband take a complete rest from his position at the brewery for a short while," he said.

"What has happened? Has he been taken ill?" Sarah Maddox said. "Let me go to him."

"I understand that he has recently been unable to supervise the men as they would expect him to," replied the doctor. "They are finding his behaviour somewhat alarming."

"In what way?"

"He seems distracted on occasions, as if in the grip of a hallucination. When these moods are upon him, he speaks in a language they cannot understand."

"Henry has no skill at languages, Doctor Voller. They must be mistaken."

"I had thought so too, until I witnessed an episode. He appears, Mrs Maddox, to be repeating some sort of Latin incantation."

—ᔕᵒᔒ—

The conservatory at Ferndown was Sarah Maddox's particular passion. "I think of it as both an extension to the drawing-room and an enhancement to the garden," she would tell her friends. The conservatory stood between the two: it could be entered from twin doors in the drawing room and via a broad glazed entrance from the garden. The glass roof was supported on iron pillars modelled on Corinthian columns capped with acanthus leaves; the space under it was dominated by a raised bed in which the centrepiece was a large tree fern. It was surrounded by a profusion of smaller ferns and palms. The walkway around it was flanked by other beds which bordered the glass walls, each home to a different species of fern, their delicate fronds set off against carefully contrived rockeries and watercourses. And upwards towards the roof the taller specimens grew in profusion, shading the silver and green tapestry underneath. A network of cast-iron pipes hidden under the raised beds maintained the glasshouse at a constant temperature between sixty and seventy degrees, depending on the season.

During his enforced absence from the brewery, Sarah Maddox sought to lift her husband's mood by involving him in the creation of the exotic plant-house. "I shall send to Mr Veitch for his latest catalogue," she said one day. "I believe that he has a magnificent range of Aspleniums – and the Maidenhair is so delicate." In normal circumstances she could expect an enthusiastic response from her husband, but her overtures now were met with an indifference which she found both baffling and hurtful.

Henry Maddox too held strong feelings about the conservatory but for very different reasons. It was there that he felt the presence of the Lady in Blue the most. He would have loved to share his wife's obvious delight in her planting, but he could hardly bring himself to cross the threshold. Whenever he stepped onto its tiled floor, he felt himself an interloper, a trespasser, unwanted and unwelcome. He was also utterly unable to explain his feelings to Sarah; they were so irrational, so counter to his usual demeanour, that he had no words to describe them. He suffered, knowing that his disposition caused deep suffering in her too.

And so night followed day, neither bringing relief to Henry Maddox. The strain was becoming unbearable, the more so because he was as incapable of resolving it as he was of understanding its cause.

"Good night, my dear, I shall be up presently." Maddox patted his wife's hand resting on his shoulder, but his words gave her little comfort. She heard the tension in his voice and felt it in his frame through her consoling touch. "Five-and-twenty to twelve is too late, and you must rest. A good night's sleep will restore you, you shall see," she said.

Maddox was sitting upright in the big library chair, awake, but with the weariness of one to whom sleep had become a stranger. "Even when sleep comes, it brings me little relief, my dear."

"What is it that is troubling you so? Last night you were crying out until I waked you."

"You do not sense what I do about this house. You cannot understand."

"My dearest, it is only a house, it cannot harm you."

"No! You have not seen her! You have not felt her hatred!" Sarah recoiled at the violence of her husband's outburst. She touched his hand, clenched tight on the leather arm of the chair. He turned and looked into her eyes. "What offence have I committed? Why does this place so resent me? What evil is lurking here?"

Sarah held back from saying what she was thinking, that the voices were of his own imagining, that the sightings were the hallucinations of – dare she admit it even to herself? – of a disturbed mind. "There is none, and you have done nothing."

"Maybe so, my dear, but I feel it in my soul, and I fear it will tear me into pieces. You must believe me. I am not mad." There. Now he had said it. The word hung between them, challenging and unresolved. She ran her fingers through her husband's hair. "I shall retire now. You will feel better by and by."

Quietly she withdrew, closed the door, and made her way upstairs. The staircase was lit from above by a bright moon shining through the glass of the atrium roof. Not yet quite full, it gave enough light to guide her steps to the landing without the need for a lamp. As the tall clock chimed midnight she settled into her featherbed, pulled up the counterpane, closed her eyes, and prayed that sleep would soon come to her and, please God, to her husband.

In the library, Henry Maddox sat quietly though he was far from being at rest. Eventually tiredness overtook him; he closed his eyes as the mantle clock struck half past twelve.

He was roused abruptly from his slumber. The sound that had jerked him awake was so unexpected that at first he struggled to place it: the long, loud blast of a whistle, close at hand. It seemed to come from inside the room, near the door. He turned his head, and his eyes fell on the undoubted source. Fixed to the wall next to the door jamb was a speaking tube, its flexible shaft covered in red silk and its flared end plugged with a small brass whistle. It was one of several in the house enabling communication between the principal rooms and below stairs. But at this time of night? Such a thing was impossible: Mrs Hedges did not live on the premises, and Fanny had long since gone to bed. The implications sent a chill of fear to the pit of his stomach. He rose, scarcely daring to answer the shrill summons.

He lifted the tube from its hook, removed the whistle and spoke into the mouthpiece: "Who's there? What do you want?" Trembling slightly, he put the open end of the tube to his ear. At first he heard a long sigh that seemed to come from afar, but then a woman's voice: close, so close it was almost in his ear; soft, and menacing.

"I am come now. I am come to do Her bidding."

Henry Maddox grasped at the door handle for support. "Who are you? Who is she?"

Again the long sighing sound, like a wave retreating on the shore.

"I am Alecto. She will be avenged."

The voice had an unearthly quality that suggested no human agent could be at work. Such was the fear gripping Maddox that he could hardly speak. "Leave me! Leave me!" he cried.

"I am come now. I will do Her bidding." The words were more distant, as if the speaker were moving away from the apparatus. And then came the chilling sound of footsteps on the stairs leading up from the basement.

Maddox summoned the courage to open the door of the library and make his way to the back stairs. All was quiet. He returned to the atrium, to the foot of the grand staircase and, still shaking, began to ascend it.

The moonlight was broken now by scudding clouds that cast shadows across the walls and floor of the vast room. The silver light played on the naked form of the statue, creating highlights and pools of shade that suggested movement in the marble itself, rather than in its source of illumination. Henry Maddox cast a glance in its direction as he reached the half landing. He was by now level with the statue's head. Slowly, it turned towards him.

Henry Maddox felt his legs weaken, and he gripped the baluster, unable to take his eyes off the horror that was unfolding in front of him. The face of the statue transformed from the serene beauty of the goddess Venus into a hideous caricature, a face contorted with rage, the epitome of malevolence. The statue's hair, braided and plaited, began slowly to turn and twist as it changed into writhing snakes, each fixing Maddox with a hypnotic gaze. With a sweep of its arm, the statue pointed towards the words carved into the pediment around the atrium: FIRMITAS, UTILITAS, VENUSTAS, the great Vitruvian precepts of commodity, firmness and delight. Maddox's eyes followed the direction of the statue's gesture. The letters swam before his eyes and changed to form new words that derided the ancient principles: VANITAS, INTERITVS, ANGVSTIA.

Then the statue spoke. The words seemed to come not from the figure but from the very walls of the house.

"Vanity, Ruin and Despair."

As the words echoed around the atrium, Henry Maddox uttered a cry that woke the household. He fell, insensible, to the floor.

18th October 1870

Dearest Eliza,

How I wish I could bring you happier news on the matter of which we spoke on Sunday. Alas, Henry is no better, indeed rather the reverse. You will recall how at the Open Day he accused poor Fanny of neglecting to inform us of a guest in the morning room, a lady dressed in blue. When we went to look, there was no-one there, and the poor girl was most distressed.

A week ago Henry was obliged to relinquish his post at the brewery until he is recovered. I must tell you now of an episode last night which brought on the most violent seizure and has confined him to his bed. He sat up late in the library, as is his wont, and though I tried to settle him, I could tell he was still troubled. After I had retired, I was wakened by the most fearful sound in the great hall, a dreadful cry. It was Henry: he had fallen on the stair at the half landing. Fanny and the girls came running, and together we managed to carry him, quite senseless, to his room. We revived him with some smelling-salts, but he was deeply disturbed, indeed delirious. I fear for his state of mind, but what has occasioned it I cannot tell.

He cried out some words to which we could attach no meaning. Florence said it was Latin (she is studying the classics in her class), but she could not decipher them. And he raved something about the statue. You will know that at Mr Westmacott's suggestion we have installed a figure of the goddess Venus in the great hall. He fancies it enhances the beauty of the room. Personally I find it somewhat overdone, and her modesty is barely concealed. But Henry would have it, and so it is there. Last night he swore it spoke to him and its face changed to that of an old crone. Can you imagine! Of course when we shone a lamp on it, it was just as it always was.

In the morning I summoned the physician, and he attended for over an hour. He reported that Henry had suffered a considerable shock, but that in his opinion he is still of sound mind. This gives me some comfort. He said that he has encountered many poor souls who have become insane, but never was their loss of mind accompanied by their gaining a knowledge of Latin. I think he meant it in jest, but it may be that he has a point. I still wonder what alarmed Henry. His demeanour is so unlike the man I know and love, and all this has happened only since we removed to this new villa. Henry says that the house is somehow to blame, but I cannot see how that can be. All I long for is to see him happy once more, but how to restore him to his former self I am unable at present to resolve.

Dearest Eliza, forgive me for burdening you so with all these troubles. Maybe when we next meet there will be better news, but though I carry hope in my heart I cannot yet see whence it will come.

Your loving sister, Sarah.

Henry Maddox's recovery from the trauma he had suffered was slow and faltering. Some days it was possible to see in him something of his former confident self; other days found him nervous, fretful, and haunted by the same terror that so recently had deranged his senses. He had as yet been unable to return to his work at the brewery, and there was even talk of his temporary replacement becoming permanent if his condition did not improve. But the house maintained its cold grip on him, playing with the composure of his mind as a cat with a mouse.

Sarah Maddox coped with the change in her husband as best she could, but she too was finding the house to be a disruptive and challenging environment. The electric bell system was proving intermittent and capricious, at times summoning Fanny to an empty room, at others to a room whose occupants had made no call for her. On another occasion every bell on the oak board at the foot of the servants' staircase had rung simultaneously, a phenomenon that the representative of the patent communication system was unable to explain or to replicate. The stove in the basement that was intended to diffuse heat throughout the house proved similarly recalcitrant, providing either too much or too little in the way of warm air, to the constant discomfort of the family. In these matters Henry Maddox, normally a man of practical skill who would rise to such challenges, was found uncharacteristically wanting: his reluctance to venture below stairs had become a topic of conversation both among his family and between Mrs Hedges and Fanny. All noticed but none could explain his behaviour; and when Sarah raised it with him, he became silent and ill-tempered.

Most days saw Maddox confined to the library where he would sit for hours in solitary contemplation. The library had the appearance of a collection that had grown over many years, perhaps reflecting the enthusiasms of several generations. The reality was that it had been created, like the garden, in the space of a few months. No sooner had the carpenter fitted the last of the mahogany book presses than the shelves were stocked with volumes that reflected the tastes of the Maddox family. For the most part these were acquired from the local antiquarian booksellers who were more than happy to furnish the room with yards of Dickens, Scott and Trollope. Sarah Maddox also prevailed upon the good nature of her father, who contributed several books from his library at Bramford on garden design and planting, and some other historical and topographical works for which he said he had no further use.

It was one of these last, a large leather-bound volume, that Henry Maddox found open on the library table one evening. Its presence took him by surprise, as it had not been there earlier in the day, and he was not aware that his wife had been in the room during the afternoon. His eyes drifted over the large type of the folio; he turned the page and froze.

What he saw was a single illustration. Its centrepiece was the statuesque figure of a lady dressed in a blue gown and attended by a gorgeously coloured peacock. From the top corner of the page stared out at him a face which he instantly recognised and from which he recoiled in horror. It was that of an old woman, grimacing, her hair a mass of coiled snakes. Maddox lowered himself slowly into the accommodating arms of a library chair. He felt his head swimming and the blood pulsing in his temples. He closed his eyes, trying to blot out the persistent image of the ghastly snaked head, trying to make sense of the other image, that of the lady in the blue dress with the peacock.

In his imagination he heard the voice that had announced the terror in the atrium, "I am come to do her bidding." She, who is she? What is it that she is bidding?

And again the voice of the old crone came back to him, "I am Alecto. She will be avenged." Avenged for what? What crime had he committed? How had he incurred her wrath? Maddox felt the silent animosity of the house, and then he spoke out loud.

"What must I do to make this stop?"

The sound of his voice surprised him and broke his haunted reverie. And then, clearly, as if she were in the same room, he heard the voice of a child, a young girl.

"Only She can make it stop."

Maddox looked round to see who had spoken, but the room was empty. He went to the door and called, "Helena!" into the echoing atrium. No reply came. His youngest daughter would be in bed at this time; besides, it was unthinkable that she could have entered the library without his noticing. He went back in and closed the door. Only she can make it stop. The voice had been close by him and carried with it the simple conviction of childish innocence. Only she can make it stop: can you not understand that? He sank back into the library chair. What was this new presence in the house? How many more unseen inhabitants did it hold?

He called out loud, "Who's there?" No reply came. He pondered what he had heard, certain that the voice had come not from within his mind, but from some external agent. And unlike that of the old woman, it had not chilled him; he had not felt fear. For the first time he could remember, he felt comforted. How a simple child could bring relief from the avenging spirit that so tormented him, he was at a loss to understand. He steeled himself to look again at the plate in the book and then turned to the text on the opposite page. What he read there enabled him, for the first time, to make some sense of his suffering. He knew now that the physician had been right in saying that he was not losing his mind, and here was the proof positive. He took a pen, and with exaggerated, deliberate strokes, he wrote his own gloss to the author's text.

Sisters

"And you say he really believes all this?"

"He is utterly convinced. And he seems unshakeable in his belief. Eliza dearest, I simply do not know what to do for the best. It is all so troubling."

The two women sat opposite each other in the morning room at Bramford Park: Eliza and Sarah, daughters of the seventh Viscount, sisters and confidantes.

"Ever since we entertained Mr Westmacott's idea of building in the Roman style, everything has gone from bad to worse. I bitterly regret having gone along with it." Sarah Maddox's manner had acquired a hardness that her sister had not seen in her before.

"My dear, you must not blame yourself. It is surely all in Henry's mind. You have nothing with which to reproach yourself."

"Since the very beginning he has suffered delusions and hallucinations. I should have taken advice sooner. Now it may be too late."

"And he imagines that he is being tormented by a – what did you call it – a frenzy?"

"A Fury. It is a mythological creature found in classical literature, I am told. He claims to have seen it, or her, or whatever it is, and it calls him up on the speaking tube from the basement and rains down curses on him."

"Poor man. And you say he showed no sign of this trouble before you moved into the villa?"

"None whatsoever."

"And you referred to another apparition. A lady in blue?" Eliza was having difficulty keeping up with her sister's account.

"She, apparently, is a goddess. Juno. She has a tame peacock which Henry has both seen and heard. On the terrace mostly. It is all so upsetting. What can have brought it on, do you suppose?"

"Could it be anything to do with his place of work? Is the atmosphere intoxicating, perhaps?"

"If it were, one would expect others to be similarly affected, and there is no evidence of such behaviour among the other employees."

Sarah Maddox dabbed her eye. It was so unlike the man she loved, and to see him go into such a decline caused her intense suffering. His condition was also becoming the subject of gossip in the town, something she found difficult to handle, and her dreams of lavish entertaining in their new home were now dashed. She braced herself to continue her account of her husband's mania.

"Last night there was another distressing episode, and I must hold myself partly responsible. Do you recall a volume from Papa's library, written by some Divine, on the county's ancient history? It has large pages with many illustrations."

Eliza pondered the question. "I can remember Papa talking about such a book, but I have never looked at it myself."

"No matter. Papa gave me the book, with several others, when I was laying out the grounds. Well, last night I discovered Henry with the book open on the library table. He had turned to a page depicting this goddess with the peacock."

"What did he say about it?" asked Eliza.

"He spoke of a visitation by another spirit, that of a young girl. According to Henry, she told him that only the goddess could bring his suffering to an end. So we have three apparitions in the house: a goddess, a Fury, and now this girl. I fear that the whole thing has stemmed from Henry reading these old books, and they have turned his head."

"You must not hold yourself responsible, Sarah, my dear. You could not have foreseen this turn of events. Has anyone else in the house seen any of these things?"

"Poor little Fanny, our maid, has become quite fearful this last month, but I believe she is being affected by Henry's moods. We have had several problems with the bells malfunctioning, and that too has un-nerved her. She has never seen the apparitions that Henry claims to see."

"And the girls?"

"I have not told them very much of what it is that has disturbed him, although they could not help but notice when we had that episode with the statue."

"And have you ever become aware of any presence in the house?"

"Not once. All I am aware of is the inconvenience of the new-fangled machinery that seems never to function as it should. In addition to the problem with the electric bells, the heating is most unsatisfactory. At times the house is as cold as ice, and at others uncomfortably warm. There seems to be no happy medium. I have spoken several times to Mr Westmacott about it, but he seems unable to resolve the problem."

Eliza sensed that her questioning was making her sister uneasy: her answers sought to divert attention away from the seemingly insoluble problem of her husband's mental state towards more practical issues that could at least admit to resolution. Eliza tried one more time to focus Sarah's attention on the main issue.

"How do you propose to proceed with – with this business with Henry?"

Sarah hesitated for some time before replying. "I believe that only a complete rest away from the house will bring him relief. But at some time we shall have to return, and when we do, it may all begin again."

"Papa has been asking after Henry. What should I tell him?" asked Eliza.

"Use your judgement. It's best not to worry him, but he must be hearing tales."

The two sisters clasped each other, and Sarah prepared for her departure. "I shall tell you of any changes, for better or for worse, my dear," she said, as she climbed into the waiting brougham.

"I shall hope for better things," said Eliza.

Sarah's carriage made its way down the long drive of Bramford Park, and Eliza watched as it receded into the distance. Her true thoughts had gone unspoken. "But I fear for the worst."

"It's too bad, Papa being so crotchety! I hate being told to be quiet all the time," said Marion, throwing down her embroidery hoop. "And I'm tired of doing cross stitch. Why can't we run round the gallery like we used to? It's too bad."

"Mama says we have to be quiet or it upsets him, and you saw what he was like last week," said Harriet.

"All the same, he didn't need to be so horrid to us." Marion's voice sounded injured, and she turned away to poke the parlour fire which flamed briefly before subsiding.

"He's very unwell. The doctor says he needs rest." Agnes, the oldest of the Maddox girls, felt the need to defend her father, though her patience too was wearing thin with the new regime imposed on the five girls by their mother.

"I can't even do my piano practice. Mrs McLeod was cross with me last week for not learning my new piece," said Florence.

"And what's Christmas going to be like this year? Mama says we can't have a party, and Papa used to be so jolly with us at Christmas," said Helena.

At eight years old, Helena was the youngest of the Maddox girls by a margin of four years. She had fair hair that tumbled over her shoulders, and bright blue eyes that took in every detail of life around her. Twelve-year-old Marion was lean and athletic, and already more than capable of beating her older sisters at tennis. Florence, fourteen, was usually content to let her: shy and slightly awkward, she was happy to follow where the other girls led. Harriet, sixteen, and Agnes, seventeen, were becoming young women faster than their parents were prepared for; the young men of Weyford were jostling for the elder girls' attention, and their presence at balls and soirées was much in demand. But on this late autumn morning the five girls were obliged to make do with their own company, and the strain was beginning to show. Mrs Maddox now discouraged visits from friends, partly to protect her husband from the noise that invariably accompanied them, and partly to protect the family from the inquisitive gaze of Weyford society. And so it was, with the late November rain cascading down the French windows, that the five Maddox sisters found themselves once more together, alone.

"So what is the matter with Papa?" Helena had none of the inhibitions that the older children might have felt concerning their father's state of health, though the question had occupied all their minds. Now it had been asked.

"He has started seeing things," said Harriet. "And hearing things, too. Things that aren't really there."

"What sort of things?" asked Helena.

Harriet felt that she had already said more than she should and tried to deflect her sister's line of questioning. "Mama thinks he had been working too hard, and that made him upset."

"Yes, but what sort of things does he see? And if they're not really there, how can he see them?" Helena persisted.

"Fanny says that he hears voices in the library," said Florence. "And you remember that night he thought the statue had come to life. That was very scary."

All the girls remembered that night: their father's expression as he lay, semi-conscious, on the staircase was etched in their memory. Agnes tried to calm their fears. "The doctor said Papa's mind is still sound."

"So, he's not making it up, then?" said Florence.

"What do you mean?" asked Marion.

"Either Papa is ill, and the voices are in his head, or he is well, in which case they must be real." Her logic was irrefutable, and it was not lost on the other four girls.

"So, maybe there is something in the house," said Marion.

"What, like a ghost?" said Helena.

"You only get ghosts in old houses," said Agnes. "Ours was only built last year. It can't have any ghosts. Not yet, anyway."

"But we don't know, do we?" Helena replied.

"There's one way to find out," said Harriet. "We can hold a séance."

In the morning room at Bramford Park, Eliza opened her desk, took a sheet of paper and began to write.

26th November 1870

"My dear sister,

I have been giving thought to the matter of which we spoke last Thursday. Like you, I am distressed beyond words to see Henry in such a distracted state, and I fear that his mania can only worsen unless he is removed from its apparent cause.

As you requested, I have spoken to Papa and told him a

little of what has occurred, though not so much as to alarm him unnecessarily. He was, naturally, shaken by the news, but last night he came up with a practical proposal that I offer for your consideration. As you know, our family has long had considerable commercial interests in the West Country; these are now managed by his cousin Sir James Melhuish. His chief interest and source of revenue has been in the export of goods to India, and latterly the victualling of the Royal Navy. Papa believes that Sir James might be able to find an opening for Henry, once he is fully recovered of course, in the exporting of ales to the colonies through Plymouth. Henry's knowledge of the brewing industry and its products might prove invaluable in such a situation.

It may be that you could persuade Henry to take a holiday in Devon in the hope that his condition improves, and if all is well Papa could arrange an introduction to his cousin. Dearest Sarah, please give some thought to this suggestion, and let me know your mind.

I remain your ever-loving sister,
Eliza."

Two days later, she received a reply from her sister.

"Dearest Eliza,
I am greatly obliged to you for your kind intervention, and to Papa for his proposal. When the moment is right, I will suggest to Henry that we both need time away from Weyford,

and the idea of visiting the West Country is appealing. But we must proceed slowly and carefully; at present the smallest thing can cause Henry to fly into a passion, and I have the girls to think of too. I will keep you informed of any progress in the matter.

> *Your loving sister,*
> *Sarah."*

THE SÉANCE

As a cure for boredom, the idea of a séance could hardly have been improved upon. The five Maddox girls set to planning the event with thrilled enthusiasm.

"We shall all sit round in a circle, and place our hands on a table, and one of us must ask, 'Is there anybody there?' and if there is, the spirit knocks on the table, and sometimes there are trumpets, or lights flickering," Harriet said breathlessly.

"And it has to be dark, so we must do it after tea," said Marion.

"Where shall we hold it?" asked Florence. "What about in the library?"

"No, Papa is always in there." Harriet thought hard, and then inspiration struck. "I know. We shall hold it in the tower room."

The tower room was a favourite place for the girls. Its arched windows looked out in four directions over the Surrey landscape, and being the only room at the top of a single flight of stairs it had the advantage of remoteness from the everyday life of the house. It had the added appeal of an air of mystery, since the ceiling was formed in the shape of the domed roof, painted with stars against a dark blue background to resemble the night sky. Sounds made in any part of the room were reflected back by its curvature with a distinct, percussive echo.

"The tower room! It's the perfect place!" said Florence, clapping her hands.

"We shall need a medium," said Agnes. "There's always a medium at a séance."

"What's a medium?" asked Helena.

"It's a person who is in touch with the spirit world. They say things like, 'Does anyone know someone called Arthur? He has a message for them,'" – this in a suitably sepulchral voice from Agnes.

"We don't know anyone who could do that," said Marion.

"Then we'll have to do it ourselves. Who wants to be a medium?" asked Harriet. No-one spoke. "All right, we'll take it in turns."

"But I won't know what to do," Florence demurred.

"Yes you will. You just have to sit there and wait." Harriet would not be gainsaid.

A date was set for the following Tuesday when Mrs Maddox's philanthropic mission met.

Helena had the last word. "And if there is a ghost in the house, we can ask it to stop whatever it's doing to Papa, can't we? And then everything will be all right again."

—◈◈◈—

"Hurry up, Florence, Mama will be back in an hour!" Marion urged her sister on as they climbed the stairs to the tower room. The spiral stair led off the galleried first floor of the villa and was accessed through an arched opening which added a sense of theatre to the curving flight of steps. Florence hung back, climbing slowly, still unsure of what they were embarking on and what her role in it should be. Once inside the room they closed the door and lit a candle. Its flame was reflected in the four tall windows and enhanced by the light of a full moon rising in the eastern sky, which cast long shadows in its silver light.

The room was panelled in oak, with cushioned window seats extending round its entire perimeter. A Persian rug patterned in red and blue covered most of the parquet flooring, and in the centre of the room was a round table draped in a heavy cloth, with six chairs spaced round it. The arched windows were flanked by classical pilasters, above which ran a circular cornice supporting the dome. Harriet placed the candle in the centre of the table, and the stars depicted above glinted in its light, the dark blue of the dome's background receding so that an innocent eye might almost be fooled into imagining the painted hemisphere as the firmament itself.

The girls arranged themselves around the table, moving the sixth chair to the north window which overlooked the terrace. The candle burned steadily, illuminating their faces brightly against the darker space behind each of them where its light did not reach.

"Now, we place our hands on the table, like this," said Harriet, extending hers in front of her. "And we have to be very still and quiet."

"What happens then?" asked Florence.

"We wait and see," Harriet replied. "If there is anything here, we can ask questions, but we mustn't move. Now, close your eyes." Marion stifled a giggle and was reprimanded with a "Shhh!" from Agnes. For a while they sat in silence punctuated by the ticking of a marble clock. The familiar noises of the house did not reach this room, and what sounds there were came from outside: an owl in the trees; a vixen calling to her mate; a dog barking in the distance.

And then, from inside the room, came the sound of a voice, quiet and close by, halfway between a sigh and word. "*Aaahh.*" Silence followed, for what seemed like an age, until Agnes spoke.

"Is there anyone there?" Silence again, and then a voice, this time distinct, and low.

"So you have summoned me. I have answered your call."

There was a collective gasp. All had heard the voice, and they opened their eyes to see who, or what, had spoken. At first their eyes, unaccustomed to the bright candle flame in front of them, did not resolve the darkness

beyond their circle. Gradually it became clear to them
that there was a new presence in the room. The sixth chair
was no longer empty. It was occupied by what appeared
to be the figure of an old woman. Hooded, and clad in
dark raiment, the creature appeared insubstantial, the
clothes assuming a human form with no evidence of a
wearer within: it had shape but not substance. The
apparition turned its head turned towards the group of
children, and within the hood a grey face, lit by the moon,
slowly resolved itself. It fixed them with a baleful stare.

"Who are you?" asked Agnes, almost in a whisper.
The creature's lips barely moved to articulate the words;
it was the voice of an old woman.

"I am Alecto. I am the agent of nightmares, the
bringer of torment, the harbinger of despair."

The old woman's words whirled in the minds of her
young audience. In the grip of their fear, they were held
captive, unable to move. Harriet found the courage to
interrogate the spectre.

"Why are you here?"

"In the shattered floor of the temple, in the ruin of
her throne, there you will find my anger. I shall blast this
house with curses that will bring anguish to its creator,
and it shall not stand. None shall here inherit."

The Maddox girls listened, dumbstruck, to the
harsh, grating utterance. Its message was largely un-
intelligible to them, but they all understood the menace

and the vehemence with which it was delivered, and they were afraid. As the reverberation of the ancient curse died away, Helena erupted in anger, rounding on the figure in the chair.

"Whoever you are, leave us alone! Leave my Papa alone! Whatever it is, stop it now!" Her voice rang out and lingered in the darkness of the room. The girls stared first at Helena, then at the seated figure, which spoke one last time.

"I shall not desist. I must do Her bidding. She will be avenged."

With those words, the face of the creature faded. At the table, Florence stiffened and drew several deep breaths before speaking. Her voice, when it came, was that of a young girl, though distinct from her own and uttered in a calm, level tone. The sound was thrown into the bowl of the great domed ceiling which echoed it back, as if the source were in the stars themselves.

"Alecto will not harm you. Her fury is reserved for those who have offended here. Your innocence is your defence and shield."

Her voice went some way to calm the fear in the hearts of the girls, and when they looked back at the chair it was empty. Marion spoke.

"Who are you?"

"I am your guardian spirit. I will protect you from her."

"Can you tell her to stop what she is doing?"

Florence's spirit voice continued.

"We are but servants of the great one. Only She can make it stop."

"Who is she?" asked Agnes, her voice still unsteady but controlled. There was a long silence. Florence drew breath, and the voice spoke again.

"She is in the motion of the stars, and in the waxing and waning of the moon. She is destroyer and protector, the bringer of life, the avenger of wrongs. She will bring you into light."

Florence sank back into her chair, released by the spirit. As the child's voice died away in the curvature of the dome, the light from the moon seemed to grow, and Harriet turned towards the window. "Look!" she cried, and the four girls followed her gaze. On the balcony beyond the north window stood a female figure clad in a blue gown, tall, majestic, and clearly visible in the moonlight. Slowly, the figure turned, and in her gaze each of the five girls felt the power of her presence. Whatever fear they had felt now deserted them, and they stood, captivated by this new manifestation.

The spell was broken by the sound of the door to the tower room being thrown open. Mrs Maddox strode in. The five girls wheeled round as she confronted them.

"Girls! So this is where you have been! What have you been doing? We have been searching high and low!"

Sarah Maddox's anger was tempered with relief at discovering her children safe. Helena turned back to the window, but of the Lady in Blue there was no sign. The window was bare; the balcony beyond, empty.

The five girls followed their mother down the steep spiral staircase to the galleried atrium, and thence to the drawing room. All were too frightened to give an account of their experience: that would have to wait until the next day, and even then their stories were wild, and at times contradictory.

Though it was clear to Sarah Maddox that all had been through a traumatic experience, she found it difficult to make any sense of their accounts. One thing, however, became immediately apparent. Whatever was the cause of her husband's torment, it had its origins in the house and not in the man. It was a revelation that would cause her to re-think every aspect of their life at Ferndown.

20ᵗʰ February 1871

My dearest Eliza,

How it grieves me to be writing for the last time from the villa we had hoped to make our home for years to come. But it must be. The malign influences that have affected Henry and now, it seems, our girls, must not be allowed to triumph, and our leaving seems to be the only way out. I am pleased to hear that the girls have settled in at Bramford, and of course you know how grateful Henry and I are to you for accommodating them while we arrange things here.

As I write this, the men from Traynor's bookshop are dismantling the library ready for the sale of the books. I think it is for the best. Henry must have no reminders of his troubled time here. We shall take some of the furniture, and the rest will be consigned for sale.

Next week we shall take our leave of this place and make the journey to Plymouth. We are hopeful that Henry will make a full recovery in a new place. The success of his introduction to Sir James has encouraged me to think that all may be well.

I shall write again when we are ready to receive the girls in our new home.

I remain, as ever,
Your loving sister,
Sarah.

THE PAST

1910

—◈◈—

THROUGH THE LOOKING-GLASS

My name is Lucy. I am ten years old. I have two brothers, Frank and Peter, and a rabbit called Nutmeg. We live in a big house near Weyford. I like our house. It has big windows, and outside there is a tennis court and a lawn where we can play. Papa goes to London every day on the train. He works at the Stock Exchange. When Papa comes home, he always reads to me when I am in bed. Last week he read me a book about a girl called Alice who goes through a looking-glass into a magic world. My best friend is also called Alice. She lives in our house, but I am the only one who can see her. She is very pretty. She has dark curly hair. Her eyes are not the same colour as mine which are blue. Hers are a sort of greeny-grey. Alice lives on the stairs, behind the mirror, but I don't think she's the same Alice as the one in the book. My Alice has a pet snake which she sometimes wears round her neck. It looks quite scary, but she says it is tame.

We have a maid named Lottie. Lottie is short for Charlotte. I told Lottie that I saw the Blue Lady last week, and she believed me. Mama says there is not a Blue Lady, but I know she lives here, and Alice says so too. I wonder if she is like the Red Queen in the book. She played croquet with flamingos, which are birds. The Blue Lady has a bird too, but it's not a flamingo, because they are pink, and this one is blue and green with a long tail which it spreads out like a fan. Alice says it is a peacock. Sometimes it stands on the terrace. It is very pretty, but it makes a horrible noise.

My favourite room in the house is the drawing room. It has a fireplace on one side, and on the other side you can walk straight into the conservatory. There are lovely plants in the conservatory. Papa says they usually grow in hot countries, but we can grow them here because the glass keeps them warm. In the middle is a palm tree. Sometimes the Blue Lady is in the conservatory. I expect she likes the warmth too. Our piano is in the drawing room. Mama says I can play quite well, but I'm not as good as her. She plays the piano after I have gone to bed. I like listening to her. In the summer we keep the French windows open, and you can go into the garden without having to go through the hall. We have deckchairs in the garden when it's sunny, and I can let Nutmeg out on the lawn, but we have to be careful because the dogs might chase her.

When I stand in front of the mirror, I can see my reflection. Behind me is the big hall and the stand where Mama says there used to be a statue. It's not there now, but I don't know why. The funny thing is, when I look in the mirror I can see a statue on the stand. It's a woman, and she's wearing a jacket with a belt, and a long dress, and she's holding a spear. I'm not going to tell Mama about her. Last time she was very cross and said I was making things up, but I know I'm not. I wish I could go through the mirror. Then I could see for myself if she really is there.

The other thing that's funny about the mirror is that I can see people in it who aren't in the house. When I see them, I try turning round very quickly to see if they're in the room, but they never are. They wear different clothes, not at all like my dresses. Alice says they are household gods, and they will look after us if we are nice to them. Frank and Peter teased me today about the mirror. They said a mirror can't reflect things that aren't there. Peter is doing science at school, and he says that light bounces off a mirror and that's what a mirror is. But I know this one is different. It's a magic mirror. Papa asked me about the Blue Lady and the statue, and I told him. He said it was probably only a dream. I'm glad he wasn't cross like Mama was. But I don't think he understands. Lottie says that grown-ups don't see things like children do. I wonder if I will be like them when I grow up.

I was talking to Alice this evening when Frank came up the stairs and laughed at me. He said, "Talking to yourself is the first sign of madness." I said I wasn't talking to myself and pointed to Alice in the mirror. He said, "Don't be silly, there's no-one there." But there was. It's just that he couldn't see her. Alice says that only very special people can see her, and I'm one of them. I think I'm very lucky to have Alice as a friend.

Tonight something is different. Papa did not read to me. He came into my room and kissed me goodnight and went downstairs. There is something wrong. I can hear their voices. He and Mama are arguing, and Mama is very upset. I think it's because of me.

Penelope Ramsden rounded on her husband as he walked into the drawing room.

"So, what nonsense have you been putting into Lucy's head, Thomas? The poor girl is behaving most strangely."

"I have no idea what you are talking of, my dear, and still less what it is to do with me."

"That book you have been reading her – *Through the Looking-Glass* – it has quite gone to her head. She spends half the day sitting in front of the mirror talking to a girl she calls Alice. And then she tells me that she can see people in the mirror that aren't there. I won't have you upsetting her like this. And Frank and Peter are disturbed by it too. It is too much."

"She has a vivid imagination, Penny, and she is acting out her thoughts. You should be happy that she is so creative and gifted, instead of finding fault."

"Happy! When all she can talk about is Red Queens and Blue Ladies and peacocks and flamingos and such! The girl is half off her head with it. And what's more, she seems to believe that there are strange presences in the house.   She was going on about household gods yesterday. Where did that come from? And then there's Lottie almost refusing to go down to that awful stinking basement.   She says there's a ghost down there, and I wouldn't be surprised if she ups and leaves, like the last girl did. How am I supposed to run a household with all this going on?"

"Please calm down, Penelope. This is wild talk, and it serves no purpose to get so emotional. I spoke to Lottie yesterday, and she seems calmer. And the air down there is better since I opened the ventilation more. It's up to us to rise above this and set an example. Getting hysterical about things won't help."

"Thomas, I am not getting hysterical. When I see people getting upset, and things going on that I don't like and don't understand, I think I have a right to ask for your support. And just now I am not seeing very much of that from you."

Penelope Ramsden turned her back on her husband and began to shake silently with tears of anger, frustration and, though she would not admit this to herself, fear.

"Please, my dear, don't take on like this. I shall speak to Lucy tomorrow, and I am sure it will be all right."

"Thomas, just leave me now. Please leave me."

Thomas Ramsden left the room and closed the door quietly behind him. He stood for a while in the large open space of the atrium staring up into the mirror that reflected the room back on itself. He could see nothing in it that came close to Lucy's imaginings, and after a few minutes he went into the library where he poured himself a large whiskey. He would talk to Lucy tomorrow and maybe start reading another book. Perhaps she would like Louisa May Alcott or, what was that new book Stewart Brown at the 'change had recommended? Ah yes, *The Wind in the Willows*. That might be better than *Through the Looking-Glass*.

His wife sat silently in the drawing room, her mind still in turmoil from the altercation. She knew that what she had said wasn't fair on Thomas, but she found herself unable to articulate her true feelings. Lucy, the little girl they had adopted as a baby, was becoming a stranger to her; her behaviour was inexplicable, and she seemed to know something that she, her mother, could not understand. Whatever it was, it was to do with the house. Perhaps Lottie was right, perhaps it was haunted; in Lucy's imagination it was filled with all kinds of strange presences: a lady in a blue dress on the terrace with a tame peacock, and all those gods and things in the mirror in the atrium. Penelope found it hard to go up the main staircase these days for fear that she too might see something there, but eventually she made her way upstairs. Thomas was still in the library, and by the time he did retire she was asleep, and their earlier angry words went unresolved.

The sound of the raised voices in the drawing room gave grim pleasure to Alecto. She preened herself for sowing discord between husband and wife. But there was so much more to be done, and no time to lose. Her eyes narrowed as she thought of Lucy. It was time to tear her from her family and use her to drive them all from the house. Time to tear her from the protection of the great goddess. Then she, Alecto, alone would have Her favour. Now the destruction could begin; now the command of the goddess could be fulfilled; now surely she would have the reward she so richly deserved.

While the sun was still low in the dawn sky, she climbed the stairs from the basement, crossed the atrium, and passed through the giant silvered pane of the mirror to the other side. For several minutes she concentrated on her transformation, and when it was complete she took her place near the statue and waited. When Lucy came looking for her friend, Alice would be ready.

"If I were you I would not be too hard on Lucy, Mrs Ramsden. Children often go through a phase of having an imaginary friend. Sometimes they will seem more real to them than their real friends. It almost always passes after a short while, and they grow out of it. I've seen many similar instances in my work, and none of them have come to harm."

Penelope Ramsden was not comforted by the doctor's advice. She could remember as a child having her own imaginary friends, but Lucy's behaviour seemed to her altogether different.

"She seems to learn things from this friend that she couldn't possibly know or find out about," she said. "The other day she started talking about Roman villas and household gods. She couldn't have learned about those things anywhere else, could she?"

"Well, those things are in books, and she is an avid reader – you told me so yourself. Perhaps she did find out about the Romans in a book. She might not remember doing so, even if you asked her. And your house is built like a Roman villa, isn't it?"

"And what about the maid saying the house is haunted? Isn't that part of the same thing?" Penelope Ramsden's voice sounded tremulous, on the edge of tears.

"Now that is definitely not part of my expertise. For that you would need to talk to the Reverend Legge. I'm sure he'd be glad to help. One more thought, Mrs

Ramsden. Maybe you should consider taking a rest, perhaps a short holiday. Often getting away from a problem puts it in perspective."

"You're beginning to sound like my husband. He said I was getting hysterical. But I'm not. I'm worried, that's all."

"Sometimes even talking about it helps. Let's see how things are next week, shall we, and in the meantime make sure you get plenty of rest."

Penelope Ramsden rang for Lottie to show the doctor out. She remained seated in the morning room, silent, pensive, and unconvinced by the doctor's recommendations.

At first I do not see Alice in the mirror. Then she peers out from where she has been hiding, behind the statue. She is laughing.

"Did you think I had gone away and left you, Lucy?" she says. "You know I'd never do that. We'll always be best friends."

"What will happen when I grow up and don't live here anymore?" I ask her.

"We will stay together. Best friends for ever." She runs towards me and stops right in front of me. "Would

you like to come this side of the mirror? I've got something special to show you."

"But I can't. Papa says *Through the Looking-Glass* is
a made-up story, and Alice didn't really go through the
mirror. It was all a dream."

"This isn't a dream, is it?" says Alice. "Here, hold
my hand." And she puts her arm out towards me, and it
goes straight through the glass just as if it isn't there. I
take her hand, and she pulls me towards her. She is very
strong.

"No, I don't want to," I say, but I can't stop myself,
and I almost fall over, and she catches me in her arms.

"There, that wasn't difficult, was it?" she says.

The room is strange. Everything is back-to-front,
even the letters round the gallery. I turn round and look
towards the mirror. I can see the real room, our house. I
know it's our house because there's no statue. Mama is
in the big hall, and I see her walk into the drawing room.

"Can she see me, like I could see you?" I ask.

"Only if I want her to," says Alice.

"I don't want her to see me!" I say. And then I hear
voices all around me, like the sounds I hear at night in the
house. It is the spirits in the walls. They are talking, and
I know they are talking about me. I try to hear what they
are saying. They sound very angry.

—❧—

There was consternation among the household gods. Their unhappiness ricocheted off the walls of the atrium, the world beyond the looking-glass, into which Lucy had been dragged by Alice.

The Head Lar, a young man dressed in a short girdled tunic, caught the mood of the domestic deities. "What's she doing here? A mere mortal among us gods – it's a proper liberty, that's what it is. She's got no right to be here. It's an insult to us all."

"For too long we have been insulted and ignored in this unholy place. Where are the sacrifices, where the libations, where the offerings that are our due?" The chorus of the Penates was petulant and shrill. "For forty years we have guarded the pantries and the wine cellars: forty years of toil, gone unremarked and unrewarded. And now the godless unbelievers send their child into our midst, to trample on our hallowed floors, and dishonour our sacred space. They must be made to pay!"

The Lares echoed the grievance. "The paterfamilias does not respect us. What rites does he perform? Where is the Lararium, where is our shrine? Where is the pot of gold with which we should be honoured?" The Head Lar threw down a silver goblet on the floor of the atrium in disgust. "When did that last see any wine? We haven't had a single offering in this god-forsaken villa. Tell me one reason why we should protect this thankless family. Especially her."

Lucy sat silently through these tirades, her eyes growing wider as each god emerged from a different corner of the atrium. They formed a circle round her and the slender form of Alice, her friend. She, surely, would defend her: was it not she who brought her to this place, this other world that was like – and yet was so not like – the world that she had left? But Alice was strangely silent, her eyes avoiding the penetrating glares from the household deities. At last Lucy could stand it no longer. She turned to confront her accusers.

"It's not my fault! I didn't want to come here! She pulled me, and I fell through the mirror. And now I want to go back!"

At this, the gods recoiled and turned to look at Alice, and back to Lucy. From behind them a new voice spoke out, "Leave the child alone. She is right." A tall figure, dressed in a long robe, swept through the atrium, stopped in front of Lucy and turned on the assembly. "Do you not recognise her? Do your eyes not tell you anything? It is you who should honour her, not she you! Were she just a mortal, do you think she could even see you, let alone sit among you in this hall? Have you forgotten the wrong that was wrought here, the desecration of the temple of the great goddess? Shame on you for your disrespect! Come here, my child."

Lucy rose and crossed cautiously towards the figure. "Who are you?" she whispered.

"I am Vesta, goddess of the hearth. I look after your home and make sure the fire is always burning. I protect all women in the household and young girls, like you."

"Do you protect Alice too?" asked Lucy.

"I do not acknowledge her. She is not one of us. Come forward!" This last command was to Alice, who had contrived to make herself as inconspicuous as possible behind the statue. "Come forward, and show yourself for what you are!"

Alice slunk out from her hiding place and stood in front of the imposing figure.

"But she is my friend! She talks to me every day!" Lucy's cry of dismay was also written in her face, crestfallen and bewildered.

"She is nobody's friend. She is false from the top of her head to the soles of her feet. Show us your true self, Alecto!"

At this, the assembled Lares and Penates, the gods of hearth and home, drew back in anticipation of the horror that was to come. Alice was changing in front of their eyes. Her hair grew matted, and acquired a motion of its own, twisting and turning, as the locks turned into snakes that writhed and hissed around her crown. Her young face became that of an old woman, cadaverous and pale, the thin bloodless lips drawn back to reveal a toothless mouth. Her young body became crooked, the arms shrivelled and the legs bent with age. The physical transformation was matched by a change of expression to a mien of pure hatred, visited on the entire company and beyond. She turned her gaze to Lucy, her eyes small red pinpoints.

"I want to go back. Now!" said Lucy.

"You shall never go back. You are mine. You will stay here with me for ever!"

"Who are you? Where is Alice?"

"There is no-one here called Alice. I am Alecto. I am your worst nightmare. I shall haunt you for ever! You will never be free of me!" Her voice grew ever louder, and higher.

Alecto had long prepared for this moment, and everything was now in place. The scenery was set; the cast assembled; she herself would direct the tragedy of their destruction. She turned to the mirror and cried out her mantra:

"I bring you nightmares, torment and despair. Here is no abiding stay. None shall here inherit!"

On the far side of the mirror Penelope Ramsden paused on the half landing in front of the giant mirror that reflected the entire atrium. Her attention was caught by what seemed to be a slight fogging of the glass – she must have Lottie polish it again. The fogging resolved itself into a figure – an old woman, almost human, but of such terrifying menace that she could not look at it for more than a second. And beyond the figure was a scene that sent a chill to her heart's core.

Reflected in the mirror was the same room, the central atrium of Ferndown with its grand staircase and gallery, but unrecognisable from the warm, well-lit space in which she was standing. The reflected image was one of total dereliction, the room now ruinous and open to the skies. Gone was the gilded lantern with its gaily coloured glass, gone the oak pilasters of the staircase, gone the tapestries and pictures on the walls, and gone, too, the doors and window frames, the swagged curtains and the polished floor. All vestiges of habitation were absent: the room stripped bare, the floor and stairs reduced to their concrete core, the walls themselves reaching up to a roofless void. The ghostly room was lit by a wintry light, cold and flat, and a chill wind blew dry leaves into drifts against the stark grey walls of the hall.

Penelope Ramsden reeled back from the mirror. Out of the corner of her eye she caught sight of a second figure, motionless on the first floor gallery. It was un-mistakably Lucy. Paralysed with fear, the mother tried to call to her child, but no words came.

The old woman advanced to the centre of the ruined atrium and stood among the drifting leaves. Raising her hands high as if to embrace the fading light, she spoke,

and her words crossed from one world to the other: "I
bring you nightmares, torment and despair. Here is no
abiding stay. None shall here inherit!" The words echoed
off the four stark walls, harsh and forbidding. On the far
side of the mirror Penelope was transfixed by the scene
unfolding in front of her. The apparition turned towards
Lucy, and back to Penelope. She fixed her with an
unrelenting gaze and addressed the petrified woman.
Her voice was now close, almost intimate, but still laced
with venom.

> "Do not try to speak to her: she cannot hear.
> What you see before you will come about
> Because I will it. Fate has decreed this fall
> And I, Fate's instrument, will do this work.
> I am Alecto, a thing of darkness. I turn day
> To night, and life to death. And soon
> She will be mine, I will use her to sow
> Discord in this house until, divided,
> It falls to ruin. The desecrating act
> Of him who trespassed here persists,
> And still must be avenged: the goddess
> Has commanded me and I obey.
> Look now upon this scene and know
> What is to come. She who was wronged
> Will soon return, and bring destruction
> In her wake. None shall here inherit.
> For you remains a life of exile;

Outcast and dispossessed
You will become a vessel for my woe
And live as a shadow, bereft of any joy.
You too are mine, and I, Alecto,
Will bind and bear you to your fate."

The old woman turned away, waved her arms at the tableau behind her, and the mirror once more gave back its usual comforting reflection of the room in front of it. Of the old woman there was no trace. But, at the same instant, the nightmares, torment and despair began for Penelope Ramsden, never quite to leave her. With a loud cry she collapsed on the stair, her face frozen with terror.

"And you say when you went into Lucy's room, she was in bed asleep?" Dr Patterson's tone was concerned, sympathetic.

"My first thoughts were for Penny, of course," said Thomas Ramsden. With the aid of Lottie and the boys I helped her into the bedroom, and we made her as comfortable as we could, but she was quite beside herself. She kept raving about Lucy, so I asked Lottie to go and check on her. Lottie came back a few minutes later to say that she was asleep in bed, and she could see nothing untoward save the bedclothes being rather ruffled. I went to have a look as soon as Lottie told this to me, and I decided not to wake her but to send for you straight away. It is very good of you to come out at this time of night."

"Not at all, not at all. You were quite right to call me. I was slightly concerned for your wife's health when she consulted me about Lucy earlier, but I had not expected such a dramatic turn for the worse. She will need a complete rest, I would suggest, somewhere away from here. I know a good clinic where they care for people with such afflictions. In the meantime she must be allowed to rest without disturbance, and the house must be kept as quiet as possible."

"And Lucy?" Thomas Ramsden sounded anxious.

"I have seen many instances of children using their imagination to make sense of the world around them. I would not concern myself overly with her, though of course you should explain carefully to her what has happened to her mother, perhaps without going into too much detail. I shall make sure to talk to Lucy again when I visit next."

Thomas Ramsden listened to the sound of the doctor's carriage departing and prepared himself for a long and disturbed night with his wife. And after that, who could say?

—❧◦❧—

Mama is not well. Papa says she has been worrying a lot lately, so she has gone to a special sort of hospital where they help calm people down when they get upset. He says he doesn't know how long she will be away. I asked Papa if it had anything to do with me and Alice, and he said I must never mention her again. I said that she wasn't my friend, and I wasn't going to talk to her any more, and he seemed glad.

I don't see Frank and Peter so often now. They are at boarding school and only come home for exeats and in the holidays. I have a governess who teaches me at home. It is not the same without Mama. I miss her very much.

I haven't seen the gods in the mirror since that night. I think maybe it was a dream, but I don't really know. From my dream I remember the goddess Vesta. She was nice. She brought me back through the mirror, and now she has banished the old woman to the basement. She said that the old woman has more to fear from me than I do from her. I don't understand why, but I hope I don't see her again; she was very frightening. The other people in my dream, the household gods, said that I should make offerings to them, and they'll help me. I have to scatter wheat seeds, and laurel and rosemary. We might have laurel and rosemary in the garden and Nutmeg eats wheat. The Head Lar said I should offer them some wine, but Papa would be very cross if I did that.

Papa says we may have to move away. He has a brother in a country called New Zealand. He says they may go into business together, and the air would be good for Mama. That would mean leaving this house. I would miss it very much if we did.

THE SALE

'It would be difficult to imagine a more perfect spot,' thrilled the sale particulars of Ferndown, 'the situation being very elevated, with magnificent views over a wide expanse of the Surrey countryside, while possessing all the advantages of a modern Gentleman's Residence.'

Thomas Ramsden rose early, his heart heavy with the knowledge that this would be his last day in residence. Even in the early hours after dawn the air was sultry, the atmosphere leaden and claustrophobic, as it had been for the last four nights. Sleep had largely eluded him, and he felt weary before the day had begun.

'The Residence is delightfully situate, forming a prominent feature in the landscape as the house is approached from the town via a carriage drive leading off the public highway. The entrance comprises a vestibule, opening into a spacious and lofty hall, or atrium, which is continued up to the roof and lighted from a lantern elaborately ornamented with coloured glass and a cluster of gilt ferns, depending from the centre.'

He stood at the rear gallery, leaning on the massive oak handrail that ran round three sides of the atrium, the fourth carrying the grand double staircase to the ground floor. He was facing directly the vast mirror; he could scarcely bring himself to look into it for fear of what he might see reflected therein. Whatever that was, it had driven Penelope, his wife, to the edge of distraction. It was the cause of the dissolution of the house and contents and the family's emigration to New Zealand. Not surprisingly, that found no mention in the estate agent's description.

'The spacious interior of the hall, with its polished floor and gallery, doubled by reflection in a magnificent mirror, on the first landing of the staircase, presents an exceedingly cheerful appearance.'

The bedroom doors were all still closed, their occupants asleep. Soon the business of the day would begin. The agent from Secker's, the auction house, had been busy the previous day setting out rows of chairs in the atrium for the bidders, and an auctioneer's table stood on a low dais at the foot of the staircase. The sale would start with the furniture and effects and end, the following day, with the sale of the house. Thomas Ramsden descended the stairs and thumbed through a copy of the sales catalogue. At his wife's insistence, every stick of furniture, every last household item, every indoor and outdoor effect, was to be consigned for sale. "If no-one shall inherit here, then we shall leave nothing to be inherited," she had said. Her words carried the torment, the anger and the sorrow of the past year, and Thomas Ramsden knew that there could be no compromise and no softening of her resolve. She had seen things the horror of which he could only imagine, and this could be the only solution. But still it went hard with him to divest himself of a lifetime's accumulation and the house he had hoped to pass down the generations.

In the smallest bedroom, near the tower, Lucy stirred in her sleep. She too had been wakeful in the night, partly from the heat which the walls of the house seemed to retain and radiate, and partly from the sounds of the house to which she was by now all too accustomed. This last night the voices in the walls seemed to be louder, more insistent, as if talking with purpose and intent rather than with the general malevolence that was their custom. Somewhere between sleep and consciousness she imagined she heard the voice of Alecto, calling out her usual curses and raining down threats and damnation. But there was another voice, the one she heard less often, and to which she knew she should pay more attention: the fearsome lady with the peacock. If she was angry, that was important. That meant something was not right at all. She woke suddenly with this realisation and ran to the window. The terrace was deserted, the row of urns along the parapet standing like sentries, the flagstones and steps to the garden scattered with the dry brown leaves of an early, arid leaf-fall. But Lucy sensed her presence, somewhere close and threatening.

By ten-o-clock the house was busy with prospective bidders. All the principal rooms had been thrown open, and where there were French windows these were held wide to encourage the free movement of air on the still, hot day.   With catalogues in hand doing double duty as fans, the visitors toured the house. In the basement they discovered the 'patent stove which diffuses warmth throughout the house', and the channels and grilles which "convey hot air in winter, and are used for the distribution of cold air in the summer'; and they smiled at the array of Moseley's electric bells, once 'the most advanced communication system on the market'. In the ground floor rooms were displayed the furniture and carpets; the ornaments, cutlery, glassware and china; the clocks, barometers, heaters and lamps; the books, the library fittings, the gramophone and piano. The more determined made their way to the stables and coach-house, and from there down to the croquet and tennis lawns, and back up the winding paths through the shrubberies and flower borders and into the house through the conservatory, where even the dahlia tubers and begonias were lotted up and offered for sale.   The entire house had been commoditised, numbered, described and listed.

The auction began promptly at eleven and proceeded at a fair pace. Richard Secker, the auctioneer, knocked down lot after lot with practiced ease, and by mid-day lot 135, 'a blue and white Spode china vase and cover', had just changed hands for two guineas. The temperature in the atrium, despite all the ventilation that could be mustered, was uncomfortable. Yet in the mid-day heat the sun itself was masked behind towering clouds that were gathering and converging on the Surrey market town.

Lucy soon tired of watching the family's accoutrements fall under the auctioneer's hammer, and she wandered listlessly through the house. It would be strange leaving the place which she had known all her life, she thought. Would there be houses like this in Wellington? She stopped at the top of the stairs leading down to the basement. The familiar dank, fusty smell arose from it, a smell she now associated with the vengeful spirit who had tricked her into crossing from one world into another, and then done everything in her power to keep her captive on the wrong side. But she had learned much there: about the Lares and Penates, the protecting household gods; about the evil spirit that inhabited the concrete house; and about the Blue Lady with the peacock, who dominated them all. It was time to pay one last visit to her tormentor. She summoned up all her courage and took the stairs down, slowly, deliberately, trying to deaden the sound of her footsteps on the polished concrete steps.

'In the basement are the kitchen, larder, scullery and the usual offices for servants.' Lucy paused at the door of the housekeeper's room, pushed it open, and stepped inside. It appeared empty, but she discovered almost immediately that she was not alone.

THE STORM

As the late August day wore on, the sale continued sluggishly. The auctioneer struggled to maintain enthusiasm among the bidders. Some, in the heat of the afternoon, had even dozed off; no mean feat on the hard folding chairs that awkwardly supported them. Lots 210, 'a pierced brass coal box and liner, with three brass fire implements,' and 219, 'a mahogany newspaper stand', attracted no bids at all; and even the books, such as Gibbon's '*Roman Empire*, half calf, seven volumes' and Thackeray: '*Works* in 13 volumes, cloth & morocco, and six others' sold below their estimates.

Outside on the terrace, unseen by any, the majestic figure of the Lady in Blue was conducting business of her own. The southerly wind that had persisted in the upper atmosphere from the earliest hours was, at her command, recruiting to itself a cluster of seven thunderstorms that had formed over Brittany in the early hours, at about the time when Thomas Ramsden had been alone on the gallery. Slowly the storms converged and began a journey that would deliver them to the very epicentre of the goddess's displeasure. The southerly wind, of all quarters the one to fear the most; it was 'the old wind, in the old anger'. The storms gradually organised and resolved themselves into a single entity, edging ever closer to the town on the River Wey, forty miles closer for each hour that passed. One storm with the strength of seven, towering seventy-thousand feet into the upper atmosphere. Its destructive power, were it to be released in a single moment, would be far greater than the entire stock of munitions that in three years' time would convulse the world in war.

In the housekeeper's room Lucy took a handful of wheat from her pocket, and scattered it in front of her as an offering to the household gods. Then Alecto spoke.

"So you thought you could escape me, did you?" She had chosen to conceal herself within the parlour armchair, her face formed in the pattern of the fabric under the wooden arched frame, her hands emerging from the upholstered arms of the chair. Lucy knew better than to look directly at her: the gnarled face with serpents for hair, the bony hands covered in parchment-thin skin. Instead she fixed her gaze on the fireplace where stood a fire-screen embroidered with flowers.

The voice of the Fury was rasping and filled with menace. "They will all go, but you will stay here. You alone will not leave this house. Or what is left of it after today. That shall be your fate."

"Indeed I shall leave," said Lucy. "I shall spend to-night with Papa and Mama and my brothers at the Angel Hotel, and soon we shall embark for New Zealand. It is you who will remain here."

"I shall, for as long as the goddess instructs me. And you. We are bound together. She is here now. She is working on it."

"Who is she?" demanded Lucy. "And what is she working on?"

"She is your Lady in Blue. The great goddess Juno. You will find out. Quite soon now."

It was enough for Lucy. She threw the last handful of wheat directly at the chair and had the satisfaction of hearing the old woman curse her, spitting out the seeds from her toothless mouth. She ran up the steps of the servants' staircase, and turning sharp right at the top ran the full length of the atrium. The auctioneer paused briefly at the sight of the girl on her mission, then resumed his cajoling of the reluctant buyers. "Come along, ladies and gentlemen, will no-one give me three guineas? It must be worth more."

Lucy ran through the entrance hall and out onto the terrace. A hot wind was picking up the dry leaves, which rustled as they were blown around in spirals. But of the Lady in Blue there was no sign. A distant rumble of thunder startled the young girl, and she looked up at the sky. Then she saw her. High in the tower which surmounted the square entrance hall, framed in the open window with its curved top, was the figure of the lady. Her arm was extended and in her hand was a spear. From the tip of the spear Lucy could see short flashes of light reaching into the heavy laden air of the afternoon sky.

Directly above the tower, its base low to the ground but its top reaching high into the stratosphere, was a cloud unlike any she had seen before. Taken in its entirety, it resembled a vast white mushroom, the cap stretching several miles wide and curving over the Surrey landscape.   Beneath the cap were several layers, all circular like the cap, but each blacker than the last. And in the centre was the hollow stem, inside which the cloud had been whipped by strong winds into clamshell-like shapes. Beneath the cloud there were flashes of lightning, followed immediately by a clap of thunder.

To the eye of the ten-year-old girl it was alive and utterly terrifying. Without a second thought she ran back into the house, into the atrium, down the aisle towards the auctioneer's table, and full tilt up the grand staircase. In vain did her father try to stop her; she was too fast to be slowed or caught.   "Lucy!   We must have good behaviour, today of all days!" he called after her, as she ran round the gallery towards the stairs to the tower. Once in the tower room she hurled herself towards the figure, who turned and fixed her gaze upon her, anger darting from her eyes.

"Stop! I beg of you, whatever you are doing, stop!" pleaded Lucy.

"It is too late. Make yourself safe, child. There is great danger. Do not leave the building."

"Whatever you do to the house, you must not hurt the people!" cried Lucy.

"Then you must warn them. Leave me now."

Lucy needed no further bidding. She ran back down the tower stairs and onto the rear gallery overlooking the atrium. Only the auctioneer could see her, but all in the room heard her shrill, urgent voice, repeating the message from the vengeful goddess:

"There is great danger! Take cover! Don't go outside!"

A hundred heads turned towards the source of the outburst. The auctioneer paused, transfixed by the sight of a child delivering such a stark message, and with such natural authority. If any in the room were uncertain as to how they should take cover, or from what, these doubts were dispelled in an instant. From above their heads came a loud crash as the first hailstones hit the glass roof, smashing the panes with ease. Broken glass showered down, and in the same instant the entire company below rose and fled for safety under the protection of the gallery that encircled the room. The hailstorm bombarded the house with stones – few less than an inch across, some the size of billiard balls. The shattered roof of the atrium covered the chairs and floor in shards of broken glass. With the roof open to the sky, the hailstones fell into the open void, forcing the terrified crowd further into the relative safety of the principal rooms of the ground floor.

Some were to be seen cowering under the billiard table; others sought shelter under tables in the dining room and library, behind curtains, and in doorways. The house was filled with the sound of ice pounding the marble floor, exploding into fragments on impact, drumming on the gallery floors and echoing off the plaster on the hard concrete walls. The relentless percussion was augmented by the screams of the trapped onlookers. Any escape from the rooms became an impossibility as the atrium filled with splintered glass, ice and water – a deadly carpet which none could safely cross. And from beyond the drawing room came the sound of the glass in the conservatory smashing into a thousand pieces under the onslaught of the hail.

Lucy had taken refuge in one of the bedrooms overlooking the terrace, where she saw to her amazement the figure of the Lady in Blue striding its length, spear held aloft, completely unaffected by the aerial bombardment. The figure paused at the top of the steps that led to the lower gardens and turned towards the house. Raising both arms above her head, one hand holding the spear, she gestured to the cloud like a conductor summoning *fortissimo* from an orchestra. Deep within the storm her command was received and translated into deadly effect. The strong up-draught in its core sheared electrons from their atoms, charging the entire cell with vast electrical energy – a positive charge to deliver not as forked lightning, but as a thunderbolt – the greatest weapon in the arsenal of the Roman gods.

The cloud towered twelve miles high above the plateau where stood its target: the turreted villa whose concrete walls had incurred the wrath of the great goddess Juno. It was time now to give vent to the implacable anger that she bore against the pretentious pile, time to deliver her judgment. With a sweeping motion she whirled the spear above her head and pointed it directly towards the offending structure. It was time for vengeance. And in her lair in the basement, the Fury Alecto collected herself and prepared for the glorious moment of ruination she had so long awaited.

Those who witnessed the event from afar spoke of a massive bolt of lightning snaking down from the apex of the storm cloud, a phenomenon with almost the brightness of the sun, lasting not for a fraction of a second but for what seemed like ten. They described the house variously as "throbbing", "pulsating", and surrounded by a halo of electrical energy. Some said it was hard to believe that any structure could withstand such a discharge, or that any persons within could survive. Certainly none of those present at Ferndown on the day of the auction would forget the moment of the strike. Most would recollect not just the bright light that flared around the house, but also the sound: the simultaneous crack of thunder that would deafen more than a few for several days afterwards; the fizzing of the lightning in the air, which some noted had the bizarre effect of making hair stand on end; and most of all the sound of the house being shaken on its foundations. One person recalled how the house seemed to be "picked up in the air and deposited with a thump that broke all of the windows in an instant". Others described how the walls seemed to glow, as if lit from within, and for hours afterwards were too hot to touch.

Thomas Ramsden stood aghast in the doorway of the drawing room as the magnificent mirror on the stairs broke free from its mountings, fell forwards onto the half landing and shattered into fragments. He raised his eyes to the lantern suspended at the centre of the atrium. Its gilt brass frame had lost in the hailstorm the gaily coloured glass panels decorated with ferns, but it still hung high above, suspended from the remains of the roof. It could not though withstand the thunderbolt. Loosened from its support, it fell the entire height of the house onto the table from which just minutes before the auctioneer had been conducting the day's sale, landing with a crash audible even above the fury of the storm. And around the entablature of the gallery the words of Vitruvius mocked the ruined edifice: UTILITAS, FIRMITAS, VENUSTAS; commodity, firmness, and delight.

—⁊∽⊚∾—

In the basement Alecto exulted in the destruction: it had gone better than she had dared hope. The house would now be a ruin, useless and uninhabitable. But there was still one task to be completed, one more destiny to shape. "Now we shall reap the whirlwind," she cackled. Emerging from the pantry chair, she made her slow way along the narrow passage by the kitchen, up the servants' stairs and out into the garden.

The storm had anchored itself over the town and was rotating slowly about its axis. Its destructive power was far from spent. The central core of the cloud was in turmoil as warm air from the ground was whirled upwards in a spiral through its centre. Surrounded by the raincloud, the approaching tornado at its core was hidden from view to any observer; the first that any in the house would know of its existence was by the roaring sound of its funnel as it touched down to ground and tracked across the tennis court, the croquet lawn and the shrubbery, towards the villa.

Upstairs, Lucy crawled out from under the bed which had shielded her from the force of the thunderbolt. The hail and rain had abated, and it felt safe to stand by the now glassless window and look across the garden. The once-trim lawn was littered with tiles, timber slats, glass from the ruined conservatory and the remains of the garden furniture. And then, a sudden thought. Nutmeg! Her pet rabbit! Had she survived the storm? What had happened to her? "Nutmeg!" she cried, running towards the back stairs.

In the drawing room, Thomas Ramsden was the first to become aware of the imminent danger. The French windows had been torn off their hinges in the storm, and the room was open to the garden. The whirlwind was now close enough to be seen. It was rotating at a fierce speed, whipping up debris and throwing it high into the air, but its movement across the lawn was slow, almost leisurely, for such a destructive force. He looked at it with apprehension, tempered with relief that the tornado's trajectory seemed to be taking it well clear of the house. Suddenly, to his horror, he saw his daughter running across the lawn towards the stable block. She seemed quite oblivious to any danger.

"Lucy! Come indoors at once!" cried Ramsden, but the roar of the wind drowned his voice. "Lucy! Come back!" He picked his way through the broken glass of the French window and started to run across the lawn. Lucy stopped and turned, her attention caught by another figure standing in the middle of the lawn, gesturing, beckoning. It was Alecto. Lucy rounded on her. "Go away, you horrible old woman!"

From the terrace Juno heard a disturbance that she had not expected but voices that she recognised. She turned, and saw to her consternation the scenario being played out on the lawn. Foolish girl! Did I not command her to remain within? She advanced along the terrace towards Lucy.

Thomas Ramsden ran towards his daughter, unaware of the ghostly presences, intent only on snatching Lucy from the path of the tornado. Why has she stopped? Why does she not move? Who is she talking to? "Lucy! Run!"

Alecto was behind the girl. By now Lucy was aware of the danger posed by the approaching whirlwind, and she ran away from the rushing funnel cloud. Alecto summoned up all her powers. She made sweeping gestures at the mass of twisting air and watched with glee as it changed direction. Its new course took it directly towards the little girl.

Goddess and Fury arrived simultaneously as the rushing base of the tornado tore at the girl's clothing and engulfed her. Lucy was swept aloft, tossed about like a doll inside the vortex. On the opposite side of the dark column of air she saw the ghastly vision of Alecto reaching out towards her, clawing at the air. Lucy closed her eyes in dread, waiting for the moment when she would be grabbed by the Fury. The twisting motion continued remorselessly upwards, but gradually she became aware that she was being held by firm hands and that they were not those of the old woman. In the very eye of the storm she now felt safe, and when she opened her eyes, she looked down on the town and the river flowing through it, and on the villa that once was home but now stood in ruins.

The view from on high bestowed on Lucy a new understanding of her place in world of gods and humans, and for the first time she made sense of the words that Vesta had spoken to the Lares and Penates, "It is you who should honour her, not she you!"   Lucy put her arms around the figure of the Lady in Blue, and was content.

THE PRESENT

—❧◈❧—

SITE VISIT

"I hope we haven't wasted a journey. There may not be anything to see." Caroline reached for her camera bag and the file of maps and drawings on the back seat. Paul parked in a cul-de-sac lined with 1960s houses. "Well, we'll soon find out," he said.

They walked up to the turning circle, beyond which a short tarmac path led into a clump of trees. "Ferndown Avenue. This must be where the tennis court was." He flipped open a file with photographs, printouts of the satellite view of the site, and a large-scale map from the early 1900s. "There's not a lot visible from the air, but we should at least be able to see the house platform, if it's not completely covered in trees." They climbed the path and made their way towards the open space where the villa had once stood. Nothing prepared them for the sight that greeted them.

"Good Lord," said Paul. "Well I'm blowed."

They stood at the foot of a steep rise in the land, which had been clear-felled of its tree cover. Tree trunks were stacked high in several places around the site, and the vegetation had been hacked back. Immediately in front of them, high above their heads at the top of the short escarpment, was the exposed length of a long retaining wall.

"I can't believe it," said Caroline. "It's exactly as it is in the drawing." She held up the print copied from *The Building News* and compared the two. "There are the steps, and one, two, three, four pillars either side." The wall was swept round at the corners and continued for some distance, containing and defining the original site of the villa. Halfway along the wall was a projection with steps either side leading up to a terrace. They walked up the steps to where the villa had once stood. In front of them the ground had been stripped of its green cover. Small fragments of concrete were visible in the earth. "The original terrace wall, still in place, after a hundred and fifty years. Amazing."

"I bet they're going to build houses here," said Paul. At the far end of the site a driveway leading to the main road had been sealed off by a section of metal mesh fencing to which a notice was attached. He walked over and read it.

"It's a planning notice – 'Proposed erection of thirteen dwellings' – plus landscaping."

"So we've just got here in time," said Caroline. "I can't imagine they'll hang about now they've started clearing the site." They spent the next half hour photographing the acre or so of land from every possible angle, ending up back at the steps. Caroline focused her camera on the wall, and Paul pulled away some ivy. "You can see the way the concrete was cast," he said. "And it's covered with stucco, and lined to make it look like stone."

"That's what the traditionalists hated about this concrete, isn't it – making it look like something else," said Caroline. "Still, it's lasted quite well." She pulled more at the ivy that Paul had dislodged, revealing some graffiti underneath. "What does this say?"

"Looks like 'Non something, something, here's'. I can't read it." Paul brushed the earth off the wall with his hand, and Caroline adjusted her camera to take a close-up of the words. "Maybe we can work it out when we get back home."

By now the skies were clouding over, and a light rain was beginning to fall.

"Do you think we should come back another day?" Caroline asked Paul.

"I think we should. We might get some better pictures when the sun's out." And so the pair decided to make another visit, to record the site and the wall more accurately before it was swept away for the new development. "Thirteen dwellings," said Paul as they turned onto the main road. "Unlucky for some."

A week later the weather had improved sufficiently to make a second visit to Weyford feasible. The retaining wall of the terrace still dominated their view as Paul and

Caroline made their way up the steep slope to the site, but as soon as they entered the open space, it became clear that they were not alone. A section of the site had been cordoned off and marked out in a grid of white tape. Some of the grid was intersected by short trenches where five people were busily at work, scraping, digging and brushing the ground. One of them, a woman in a waxed jacket and jeans, rose from the trench and watched as Paul picked up a lump of concrete that was lying in front of the retaining wall and crossed the terrace. Her introduction was terse and to the point.

"Margaret Pearson, Surrey Archaeological Trust."

"Hi, I'm Paul Conrad. And this is my wife Caroline. We're interested in the history of this place. We've come to see what's left of the house that used to be here."

"Not much, by the look of it. But that's how things seem to go round here. We've been digging for four days and found absolutely nothing."

"What are you looking for?"

"A Roman temple. At least, the remains of one. It was here in 1760, but there's not a trace of it now. It's in Massingham, you know."

"Where's that?" asked Caroline.

"Not where," said Margaret Pearson. "Who. Ambrose Massingham. The antiquarian. He surveyed the whole county in the eighteenth century. There wasn't a single archaeological site that he didn't record – wrote them all up, mapped the sites, and now this one's disappeared off the face of the earth. It's a complete mystery. Four days' work, and all we've got to show for it is a few bits of tile and two sherds of a Samian ware biscuit barrel." The last words were thrown contemptuously at the finds table where these trifling spoils had been bagged and tagged.

"Maybe you're looking in the wrong place," said Paul.

"I don't think so," said Margaret Pearson, with an air of finality. "And we've got to be off the site by Monday. That's when the bulldozers move in. So why are you interested in the house?"

"It was built by my great-grandfather, Charles Partridge, in 1870. He was a pioneer of concrete building. It was all built of concrete."

"1870? Isn't that rather early for concrete?"

"Not really. There was quite a craze for it then. They used to cast whole houses in it. This is a picture of the one that was here." Paul pulled out a print of Ferndown and showed it to the small team who by now had gathered round their leader.

There was a buzz of interest and much pointing from the print to the level platform of earth where the house had stood. Margaret Pearson fixed her gaze on the terrace wall and turned back to Paul.

"This concrete. What did they make it of?"

"Pretty much anything they could lay their hands on. Gravel, stones, bricks. If there was suitable material on site, they'd use that first. It was cheaper than buying it in. Partridge even patented a stone-crushing machine for the aggregate."

There was a short pause while the archaeologist digested this new information. Paul Conrad felt a growing sense of unease which became tangible with her next question.

"What's that you're holding? Is that part of the old house? Let me see it please."

She took the lump of grey concrete, peered at it, rubbed it, and placed it on a flat stone. Reaching in a box of tools for a cold-chisel and hammer, she struck it hard with one well-directed blow. The concrete split into two pieces, each exhibiting a fresh un-weathered face.

The group gathered round, staring first at the concrete, and then at Margaret Pearson.

"Dear God. Tell me I'm not seeing this," she said, her voice low and suddenly intense. "Michael, what would you say that was?" she asked one of her team. He peered at the block and scratched at a pink lump in it.

"I'd say that's a piece of Roman brick. It's got just the right texture and colour."

Margaret Pearson took a sharp point and dug at another part of the concrete. From under the grey cement a small patch of blue glinted in the afternoon sunlight.

She unscrewed a water bottle and dabbed at the fragment with a wet tissue: it glowed bright and shiny.

"Sandra?" There was another pause while the second examination was conducted.

"Most probably a tessera from a mosaic. The deep Prussian blue could date it to the first century AD. Glass, of course, not limestone."

"Just as I feared," said their leader.

"So, you think they may have scooped up some of the old temple and . . ." Paul Conrad's voice tailed off as Margaret Pearson collected herself and turned slowly to address the gathering.

"Mr Conrad, if what I think is correct, we are looking at possibly one of the greatest acts of cultural vandalism of the nineteenth century. Let me tell you a little about this temple. It was one of very few in the world dedicated to the goddess Juno, and certainly the only one in England. It was circular, which makes it highly unusual in this country, and it had a mosaic floor depicting the story of Juno and the Peacock. Possibly the only mosaic ever recorded to illustrate that fable. The peacock's train was said by Massingham to be of the most fabulous greens and blues. Like that," and she jabbed venomously at the fragment in the lump of concrete. "And the figure of Juno herself was said to rival any image of her before or since."

"Ah."

"And it would appear that your grandfather . . ."

"Great-grandfather," Paul corrected.

"Your *great* grandfather is responsible for tossing it all into a cement mixer and turning it into concrete."

Caroline came to Paul's defence. "I don't suppose he did it knowingly," she said. "I mean, he wouldn't deliberately destroy a historic monument, would he?"

"It makes no difference. The result is just the same."

"At least he didn't use Roman cement," said Paul, and instantly regretted it.

"Mr Conrad, this is not funny."

"Ah, I'm sorry Ms Pearson . ."

"Dr Pearson, thank you. There's obviously no point in our continuing this exploration, so we might as well all pack up and go home. I trust you will have more success in your research than we have had in ours." This last was heavy with irony.

The two made their way back to the car in silence.

Once inside, Caroline spoke first. "That didn't go very well, did it?"

But the awful thing was, on one level it really was quite funny: the hired hands from the brewery uncaringly heaving chunks of Roman masonry and mosaic into the insatiable jaws of the stone-crushing machine, the churning of the fragments into malleable concrete. They looked at each other and burst into laughter.

—◦◦◦—

Over dinner that night, Paul and Caroline discussed the events of the day.

"It was rather unfortunate, the archaeologists being there when we arrived," said Caroline, "We didn't get any more pictures either. I suppose we'll just have to make do with what we've got."

"I expect I can brighten them up if they're a bit dark," said Paul.

"So, what do we do next?"

"I'd like to get the concrete analysed," said Paul. "They can do that at the Concrete Foundation. I could drop it off next week." Paul's research into his great-grandfather had made him a frequent visitor to the specialist library of the trade association.

"So we can find out if there really is a Roman temple mixed up in it, you mean?"

"Not only that. If we're going to write all this up, it would be good to know the mix, and all the other constituents."

"OK, so we'll drop off a sample with them and see," Caroline replied. "Do you think we should tell Dr Pearson what they find?"

"Only if we want another earful from her. I still haven't recovered from the first."

Caroline laughed. "And we should try to find a copy of that book that she mentioned."

"Ah yes, Massingham. That was funny too."

"Well, it does sound like a town, somewhere in Suffolk, I'd say."

"Actually it's in Norfolk. Near King's Lynn. I looked it up."

"What I'd like to know is why the house was abandoned," continued Caroline. "There must be someone who remembers it. I think a letter to the *Surrey Messenger* might be a good idea."

"So, lots to be getting on with, then."

"Never a dull moment," said Caroline.

Julia Fielding

Caroline's letter to the *Surrey Messenger* bore fruit in the form of a reply from Weyford. "I remember the house well. When you are next in Weyford I would be happy to tell you about it." Caroline arranged a visit for the following week. The writer lived on a tree-lined street at the top end of the town. Paul rang the bell, which prompted a furious barking from inside the house.

"Come in, come in. Don't mind Maisie." Julia Fielding ushered Paul and Caroline into her sitting room. Maisie, a Sealyham terrier, asserted herself noisily before settling down on the hearthrug. "Let's have some coffee, and then we can talk."

Julia Fielding was a retired teacher in her early seventies with a silver-grey bob. She sat leaning forward in her chair as Paul and Caroline told her about their research into Ferndown, her eyes flicking over the photographs and plans that they had brought.

"So that's why we put a letter in the paper, to see if anyone still remembered it. It was rather a long shot," Paul concluded. Julia put down the portfolio of pictures on the low table between them.

"Well, I hadn't thought about the old house in years, but when I saw your letter, I just had to get in touch."

"You said you used to live near it when you were a child?" said Caroline.

"Yes, that's right. My parents moved to Weyford shortly after the war, and I was born in 1946. Gosh, that's showing my age, isn't it! Our house was on Sandpit Lane, about a quarter of a mile away. All the local children used to sneak off and play at the old house. Strictly forbidden, of course, because it was probably dangerous. You'd never be able to do that now, with all these health and safety people, but everything was different in the nineteen-fifties."

"What was the house like?" Paul asked.

"It hadn't been lived in for years. I think the last people left before the First World War. Between the wars someone kept chickens there, I believe. Can you imagine, keeping chickens in a ruined mansion! Anyway, after the war it was left empty. Most of the windows had been broken, and the middle bit, which had obviously been quite grand, was open to the sky. It had a huge staircase which we would run up and down. We used to race each other round the gallery, which went all the way round from the top of the stairs."

"There were lots of rooms, weren't there?"

"Compared with our house it was like a palace, but I was only a child so it probably seemed bigger than it was. There was a basement which smelt awful and was very dark. We didn't like going down there. The ground floor rooms were huge. Some of them had French windows which had fallen off, so you could run in and out of the garden. And upstairs there were these lovely rooms that looked out over the North Downs – you could see for miles. It must have been a beautiful house once."

"Why do you think it was abandoned?" asked Caroline.

"I don't know. But it did happen a lot at that time – there wasn't the money to keep these big old places up. Lots of them were demolished. Such a shame."

"Didn't it frighten you, such a big empty house?"

"I suppose that's why we liked to go there, to give ourselves a fright. We used to pretend it was haunted. My sister once dressed up in a sheet and waved her arms at us." Julia Fielding gestured the motion, then paused, and turned her head slightly. "But now you come to mention it, I do remember something that really did scare us." For a moment she seemed scared all over again, and a slightly distant look came into her eyes.

"Do you want to talk about it?" said Caroline. "Please don't, if it's a bad memory."

"No, it's all right. It's just that I hadn't thought about it for years, and it's come back to me all of a sudden." She looked up, back in the present day. "Do have some more coffee."

After a short pause, during which the coffee cups were refilled and biscuits passed round, she continued.

"I would have been about ten at the time. Four of us, my sister Frances and I, and two boys who lived near us, David and Timothy Nichols, we all went to the house one Sunday afternoon. It was raining, and we ran to the house to keep dry. When we got there, we went up the stairs as usual, but because it was so wet we went on up into the tower, to the highest room in the house. It had windows on all four sides; you could see out in all directions. It wasn't a big room, but it had a lovely domed ceiling which gave it an echo – that's why we liked going there.

"I was looking out of the window. I glanced down at the terrace below, and I saw a young girl – she can't have been more than nine or ten – standing by the balustrade. She didn't seem bothered by the rain. Then she turned and went towards the entrance hall."

"What did you do?" asked Caroline.

"I pointed her out to the others, but by the time they got to the window she'd disappeared. So we went back into the main hall of the house, and there she was, on the half landing of the stairs. She had on a sort of pleated dress, dark green, with a low waistband – not at all like the way we were dressed.

"We were quite a long way away from her – right across the other side of the room, so we couldn't see her close-to. Timothy called out to her: 'Who are you?'" Julia Fielding paused briefly, marshalling her memories and summoning her resolve to continue.

"I remember this next bit well. She turned and looked straight at us, but instead of telling us her name, she said, 'You mustn't play with Alice. She's not really Alice at all. She's horrid.' Then Frances said something like, 'We don't know anyone called Alice.' And the girl said 'Alice lives here. But her real name is . . .' and I can't quite remember what she said, but it sounded like 'Electra'."

"That must have been frightening." Caroline's voice betrayed her concern for having awoken what was clearly still a potent memory.

"It was. And there was something about her voice too. It sounded prim, almost old-fashioned. And when she spoke, the sound seemed to come . . . not quite from her. I don't know how to describe it – it didn't have any sort of direction. You must think me very silly to talk about all this." Julia became flustered, and Caroline tried to calm her.

"No, not at all. I'm sorry we mentioned it. Please don't distress yourself."

"I'm fine, really. It's just that I've never spoken about it to anyone."

"Did you manage to get closer to her?" asked Paul.

"No. She ran upstairs, into one of the bedrooms. David called after her, 'What's your name?' She didn't answer, and we ran round the gallery after her. When we got to the bedroom, no-one was there. The room was empty. We did hear her voice – just one word: 'Lucy'. We heard it in the bedroom even though she wasn't there. Such a strange experience."

"Did you ever see her again?" asked Paul.

"Never. I don't think we went back to the house much after that. We pretended to each other that we weren't scared, but I mentioned it to Frances once, years later, and she confessed to me that she'd never been so frightened in her life. There was something so . . . unreal about it."

"And what about this Alice, or Electra, or whatever her name is. Did you ever see her?"

"No. And I don't know what Lucy meant by saying 'she lives here', as if she still did. That was the thing that spooked us most, I think."

There was a long silence. Caroline eventually broke the spell.

"You mentioned a film in your email."

"Oh yes. I must tell you that story. It was a few years later – probably about fifty-eight or fifty-nine, I don't know. I would have been twelve or thirteen by then, and I was at the Girls' Grammar School. I was very good at games, and my father had bought a cine camera to film me running and playing hockey. He was quite a good photographer. Anyway, one day we heard that the old house was finally to be demolished, and they brought in a firm to knock it down. When they started, apparently it was so tough that they couldn't make any impression on it. Something to do with the concrete, I suppose; you'd know more about that than I would. The next we hear is that they're going to get the Army to blow it up, with explosives.

"My father served with the Royal Engineers in the war, so he knew about that sort of thing. He contacted the regiment and asked if he could film the demolition. And to everyone's amazement, they said yes, as long as they could have a copy of the film. On the day, Dad went up there with his camera equipment, and we were allowed to watch from a safe distance. A lot of people turned up – it was quite an event. Dad said that the soldiers had spent the best part of the previous day setting charges around the house.

"He put his camera on a tripod, pointing towards the house, and when they were ready he set it running, took cover, and they detonated the explosives. There was a huge bang: it could be heard for miles. Our ears were ringing for hours after." Julia Fielding laughed at the memory.

"And you've got the film." Paul could hardly contain his excitement.

"Well, I don't know if it's still any good. It's over sixty years old." She reached into a desk drawer and took out a small cardboard box. Inside was a yellow canister, little more than three inches across, and inside that a spool of eight-millimetre film. "I'm afraid I didn't keep the projector. It was too big and heavy."

"I may be able to help there," Paul said. "I used to work in television, and I know someone who can digitise it. Would you let me borrow it for a week or two?"

"Of course. Keep it as long as you like. It's been sitting in that drawer for twenty-five years."

"I'll look after it."

They made a move to leave.

"Oh, but you must have the sound," said Julia, rummaging in the drawer.

Paul turned. "Did you say sound?"

"Yes, Dad had one of those portable tape recorders. He was very proud of it. He got it in Germany, I think. Ah, here we are." She took out another small cardboard box containing a reel of recording tape. "He used to spend hours trying to get the sound to fit with the picture. It was such a fiddle."

"Julia, we owe your father a big debt of gratitude. To film the demolition is fantastic. But to record the sound as well, that is pure genius." Paul took the second box and put it with the film. "And with my friend Bill Harrington's help, we should have no difficulty getting it to fit with the picture."

THE FRAGMENT

Paul's first thought on returning from Weyford was the transfer of the film, but the earliest date his former colleague could manage was some weeks away, so he turned to other outstanding work.   He loaded the photographs from their first visit into his computer and scanned the file index for the close-ups of the graffiti on the wall. Selecting the most promising, he set to work enhancing the images. None of the writing was clear, and he guessed it had been there for some years certainly, to judge by the growth of the ivy over it.   The words were in capital letters and covered most of one of the bays of the terrace wall between two of the sloping pilasters. Caroline entered the study. "How's it going?" she asked.

"I've only just started.   It's not very clear."   He increased the brightness of the image, and more of the paint showed through.   "That's NON at the beginning. And this word at the end, HERES – without an apostrophe, of course. Typical. But here's what? There isn't another word after it."

"The next to last word looks like CRIT." Caroline offered. And before that, is that TVNE, or TUNE?"

"The second word, that's more difficult. They look like Vs, but there's no vowel. VLLVS. That doesn't make any sense."

"If the first word is Non, it could be in Latin." Caroline offered.

"Now come on, who ever wrote Latin graffiti on a wall, apart from the Romans?"

"That would make it NON ULLUS, not NON VLLVS."

"OK, so what about the next two? TVNE? That's not Latin, and nor's CRIT."

Caroline opened her laptop and entered the words into a browser. "NON ULLUS TUNE CRIT HERES" she typed, and hit Return.

"It says, 'Do you mean *Non ullus tunc erit heres*?'" she said. "Do we?" She copied the words. "Why don't we try an online translator? From Latin . . . to English." She pasted the words into the Latin side and gave a small cry.

"Look Paul – look what it says. 'Then there will not be any heir.' That's spooky. There won't be any heir. It really does mean something."

Paul's search also had a result. "Here's the full line. It's from a fragment of Latin verse: *Nemo manere potest, non ullus tunc erit heres.*"

Caroline typed the first three words into the translator and read: "No-one can remain." She paused. "Paul, this is weird. 'No-one can remain; there will not be any heir'. That's what happened to the house. No-one lived there long, and then it was empty."

"And it gets weirder. Would you believe it's part of a poem about a Roman temple," said Paul, reading from his screen which showed a website adorned with classical images. "It's a curse.

Monstrum noctivagum ferimus, diros cruciatus;
Nemo manere potest, non ullus tunc erit heres.

Ah, good, there's a verse translation,

I bring you nightmares, torment and despair!
Here is no abiding stay. None shall here inherit!

Strong stuff."

"What does it say about the poem?" asked Caroline.

"It's a fragment that has always puzzled scholars. No-one's been able to offer any explanation as to who wrote it or where it came from. Some have suggested Virgil, but there's nothing definitive. I'll print it out. Just the English, for now."

The printer clicked and whirred into life, loaded a sheet of paper, and began to print: *The goddess Juno foresees the ruin of her temple.*

The goddess Juno foresees the ruin of her temple

High on the wings of morning flew Saturn's daughter,
Queen of the gods, of Jupiter the wife, and dam to
Mars and Vulcan: great Juno, whose relentless rage
Tormented bold Aeneas. No barriers of space or time constrain
her progress: she sets her course towards a northern land,
to where her temple, mighty and sheathed around with bronze,
and rich with offerings, once stood in splendour
on the chalk-white hills. Seeing from afar, she stops, transfixed.
Her house, within whose pillared cirque her image
burned in blue and gold, lies desolate.

       With hideous intent, the sinewed limbs
of labouring men, armed all with deadly two-edged pick,
hack at the ruined walls and scrape the tessellated ground.
Juno's fair image, the strutting peacock's fan, raked into pieces;
these plundered spoils, torn from the ancient earth, they cast
into the jaws of ghastly engines, whose mangling wheels
crush and spin the debris into crumbs.

       The goddess feels these wounds
as if inflicted on her person. Seething with anguish
she pours out her wrath: "What, am I to suffer this assault
and not avenge the crime? This cursed race of heathens
shall atone for their destruction! Are my powers diminished
by the passage of two thousand years? No! I shall summon
all my might, and they shall pay the price for their misdeeds!"
Further in time the goddess looks, and on the ground
made barren by her temple's loss she sees a villa stand.

Its walls entrap the fragments of her once-great house,
her image ground to dust, dishonoured and immured.
Down she swoops. Armed with a spear, in goatskin clad
with strutting peacock close, see her now: the mighty Juno,
warlike in aspect, and consumed with rage. She raises high
her spear, strikes the presumptuous abode, calls down on it
her curse: "I bring you nightmares, torment and despair!
Here is no abiding stay. None shall here inherit!"
She enters in and sees with loathing the pilastered hall, the
gilded stair, the mirror, doubling the insult in its reflecting pane.
Above she reads in a familiar tongue the Vitruvian tropes,
writ large around the room: *firmitas, utilitas, venustas.*
Commodity, firmness and delight. Some chance!

                                        And then the statue
she espies: "You! You whom Paris once preferred to me, and
judged the fairer: you stand now where once my temple stood!"
The ancient grievance swells within her breast. "I have
endured enough. No greater outrage could be committed here.
Venus shall not remain within these walls, and he
who set her here shall rue the day!" With that
she calls Alecto from her hellish den to do her bidding.
The Fury loathed even by her kin, she who can
assume the shape of any form, with hair of coiled snakes,
her visage so grotesque it drives men mad: Alecto,
now let loose to punish the wrongs of heedless men.
"Come, Daughter of the Night, you of a thousand names
and deadly guiles, whose hatred knows no bounds!
Perform this one last labour – do me this service now!"
Alecto rose to earth and set to work.

Film Transfer

"Bill! It must be twelve years at least!"

"Paul! And you haven't changed a bit!"

Bill Harrington's editing studios had changed considerably since Paul Conrad's last visit. Then, Paul was working as a television producer, and Bill was editing documentaries; the two had worked together on many projects. Now in semi-retirement, Bill augmented his pension by transferring reels of film to digital formats.

"This is different," said Paul. "Wasn't this the main editing room? And the Steenbecks were in there."

"I've still got a couple," said Bill. "They're still the best machine for viewing sixteen-mil. But this is what we do the transfers on. I got it for a song when they closed down at Ealing." The object in question was a large telecine machine, of the kind once commonplace in the post-production suites of large broadcasting companies. Its purpose was to scan film frame by frame and turn the images into broadcast-quality television pictures.

"I knew we'd still need them. There's no limit to the amount of film needing to be digitised."

"You canny old so-and-so. Not a bad investment, I'd say."

"It keeps me off the streets. So, what have you got for me?"

Paul handed over the small reel of eight-millimetre film and explained how he had come by it. "The great thing is that this chap even recorded the sound of the explosion. On quarter-inch." He took out the reel of magnetic tape.

"So this house, then, why did they have to blow it up? Why couldn't they knock it down?"

"It was too solid. My great-grandfather's concrete was very strong. They even used some of his houses as air-raid shelters in the war."

"So they called in the Army? It says here, the 101st Corps Royal Engineers." Bill Harrington read the label on the film's box.

"That's right. They let the chap who took the film put his camera on a tripod in front of the house. He set it running, ran for cover, and the Army pressed the button. Apparently it's pretty spectacular."

Bill Harrington busied himself transferring the sound onto a more durable magnetic track, then loaded the two spools onto the telecine machine. The tiny spool of film was dwarfed by the large round plates designed to accommodate entire reels of feature films. He threaded the narrow celluloid film through the gate, in front of the rotating prisms that would capture each frame and save them to a computer memory.

"Right – let's get the sound in sync, and we'll give it a whirl." Bill ran the film to the point of the detonation and lined up the sound of the explosion to match the vision. Then he spooled back to the beginning and ran the film.

There were fully two minutes of a static wide shot of the derelict villa before anything happened. On the soundtrack could be heard the terse communication of the Royal Engineers as they made the last preparations for detonation. Then, "Take Cover!" A few seconds pause, followed by the single command, "Fire!"

The explosion was so violent that the camera was rocked on its tripod. Plumes of debris were hurled in all directions as the villa was torn apart by the force of the detonations. The explosives had been placed at key points around the building to ensure maximum destruction. After the initial burst of flame and fire, coming from several parts of the villa, the entire building was enveloped in a cloud of smoke and dust. Large lumps of concrete fell to the ground. The sound of the explosion was equally impressive, from the sharp percussive impact of the first moment of detonation to the steady roar of the building collapsing in on itself.

The loudspeakers on the wall of the editing studio shook with the resonance.

"He must have had a good mic to withstand that blast," said Paul.

Slowly the dust settled, some being blown to the left of frame by the prevailing wind. After a long minute the result of the demolition was revealed. Scarcely any part of the villa had survived. Where before had stood the gaunt walls, windowless and open to the skies, there was now a large mound of shattered rubble. Four men in uniform walked into the shot and approached the demolished building. They surveyed the site briefly to satisfy themselves that there were no unexploded charges, and exited to the right of frame. The camera stayed running for a further minute or so, then cut off as the film ran out.

"Well, that was quite something, wasn't it?" said Bill.

"It seems such a shame, though," Paul replied. "In its time it was one of the finest examples of concrete work in the country."

"Yes, that is sad. But it had seen better days, hadn't it? Shall we go and have lunch?"

They crossed the Goldhawk Road to the pub that had been their regular haunt when they had last worked together, leaving the digitising equipment to analyse the film frame by frame, remove dust and scratches, and grade the colours to the optimum. After an hour of reminiscing the two returned to the editing suite.

"Right, it seems to have done its stuff. I'll run you off a couple of discs." Bill Harrington loaded the disc recorders and set up the transfer from the computer's memory banks. They settled down to watch the result of the processing on a large video screen.

"Do you remember that film we did on the Camargue, Bill?"

"Remember it? – I'll never forget that shot of poor old Jeremy trying to ride one of those white horses bareback. I wouldn't mind betting he's still got the bruises."

"To say nothing of – what's that?"

Paul broke off suddenly. The picture on the screen was still showing the static shot of the villa before the detonation of the explosives.

"Where did she come from?"

"She wasn't there before!"

In the foreground of the frame was the long wall of the terrace, still with its baluster rails in place, behind which was the façade of the villa. Between the low baluster and the house was a female figure walking steadily, majestically, along the terrace. She was dressed from head to foot in a blue gown.

"It must be something on the computer, Bill – you're not doing any CGI, are you?"

"Couldn't, even if I wanted to. This set-up doesn't do that sort of thing. Where's she going now?"

The figure turned her back to the camera and entered the villa. At first she could be seen clearly through the glassless window openings and then disappeared briefly.

"Good God, she's at the top of the tower." Paul's mouth was dry. "There's only a few seconds before it all goes up." The woman was now framed in the opening of a window of the topmost tower room, standing as if a statue in a recess.

On the soundtrack could be heard the same barked orders of the Royal Engineers before the final command. Then, "Fire!"

The explosion was the same as their first viewing. Once again, the dust and debris settled and the mound of rubble was revealed. Once again, the soldiers inspected the ruins. But this time, in front of them, looking straight into the camera's lens, was the imposing figure of the blue-gowned woman. On the soundtrack too there was something new. As the figure turned slightly to her right, there could be heard unmistakeably, clearly, the cry of a peacock.

"Let's have another look at the film, Bill."

Bill Harrington rewound the film and replayed it.

"Nothing. She's not there on the film. Only on the disc." He spooled the film forward to a point after the explosion. Again, it was exactly as when they had first viewed it. He removed the film from the telecine machine and unloaded the discs. Visibly unnerved by what he had seen, he moved rapidly, placing all the material in a carrier bag. When he spoke next, his voice had lost all its usual bonhomie.

"I don't know what you've got there, Paul, but I can tell you, I've never seen anything like it."

Paul found himself almost incapable of speech, and then as he took the carrier bag containing the film and discs, he said quietly,

"She's still there. She's still there."

THE CONCRETE FOUNDATION

The Concrete Foundation occupied a large building set in parkland on the southern edge of Basingstoke. It had been set up in the 1950s to promote the use of concrete in the construction industry, and to conduct research into its properties. There were those at the time who questioned why such a universally adopted material was in need of promotion, any more than eggs, milk and potatoes needed their recently-created marketing boards; but over the years the Concrete Foundation had flourished, and it was now recognised as the leading authority on all aspects of concrete whether technical, educational or historical. The public face of this august body, Desmond Pollack, was used to fielding queries on concrete construction, but on the day in question he was feeling distinctly out of his depth and ill at ease.

Paul was ushered from the reception area into a large conference room in the centre of which was a table bearing several of lumps of concrete, each numbered and labelled.

"Ah, Mr Conrad, how nice to see you again," said Desmond Pollack. He poured two cups of coffee and they sat down. "You have presented us with quite a conundrum."

Paul recognised the sample of concrete that he had

delivered to the Foundation some weeks previously, with a request for an analysis of its content. Only in this way could the truth be established as to whether, and in what proportion, the concrete contained Roman remains. "Is concrete of this age difficult to analyse?" he queried.

"Oh, no, no, not at all. That is perfectly straight-forward." Pollack handed him a paper containing a detailed breakdown of the sample with tables listing constituent parts, their chemical composition and proportions. "We see this material quite frequently," he continued, "And your sample is typical of its time. The Victorians used pretty much anything that came to hand in their concrete: they weren't too fussy about what they put in. Broken bricks, old plaster, coke breeze from the gasworks, you name it. It's not unknown to find old boots and shoes in concrete of this period, though your great-grandfather seems to have had a better grip on quality control than some."

"That's gratifying. What about the Roman temple theory?" asked Paul.

"Ah yes, that's certainly true. We found several pieces of crushed brick which we sent for analysis, plus some fragments that appear to have come from a mosaic floor. All came back positive: there's no question about that. Whatever was left of the Roman temple seems to have made its way into the walls of the concrete villa."

"So what's the conundrum?" Paul asked.

Desmond Pollack shifted uneasily. He was a man who was used to dealing in certainties, and he liked to provide answers to questions. Today he was unable to do either.

"It's not about what went into the concrete, Mr Conrad, it's what's happened to it afterwards that we are finding problematic. Let me try to explain." He picked up one of the lumps of concrete that had been sawn in half, leaving two clean faces revealing the interior. "The Victorians, and your great-grandfather was no exception, had a limited knowledge of the properties of concrete, and in those early days they experimented by adding iron to strengthen it. Usually it was hoop-iron, which is simply strips of iron used in the making of barrels. The coopers, the barrel makers, bound together the wooden staves with hoops of iron, hence the name. In concrete it was used as an early sort of reinforcement, though it was to be some years before any real calculations were done on how reinforced concrete actually behaves." He paused, took a deep breath, and continued nervously. "In all of these samples, we find that there is no hoop iron remaining."

Paul peered at the surface of one of the samples. "So what's happened to it? Has it rusted away?"

"No. It would appear to have been subjected to extreme heat. It has not just melted, Mr Conrad, it has been vaporised."

"Maybe there was a fire at the villa?"

"It's more complicated than that. In a house fire the temperature typically reaches about a thousand degrees Celsius. Iron melts at just over fifteen hundred degrees. Now, concrete acts as a fairly good thermal insulator, so it protects any iron or steel inside. And because concrete doesn't conduct heat well, the reinforcement tends not to deform greatly – I'm generalising here, you understand. So in a typical house fire, the temperature at the centre of the concrete wouldn't normally be high enough to even melt iron, let alone turn it into a gas. To do that you need temperatures nearing three thousand degrees Celsius."

"How do you know there was any iron there in the first place, if it's not there now?"

"Quite simply because it is still there. When we looked inside the first sample – the one you brought us – it was obvious that the concrete at the centre had at some point become very, very hot – hot enough to turn the sand, the silicates, into glass. Some of the concrete had vitrified. At first we thought maybe this was some glass that had been mixed in with the aggregate, so we sent someone to the site to collect a few more samples. He got there just before the builders laid it all down as hardcore for the driveways to the new houses. He collected several pieces, as you can see, and almost all of them exhibit the same thing. And when we analysed the vitrified centre, we found it contained a high proportion of iron – the hoop iron had been literally vaporised and blasted into the concrete."

Desmond Pollack paused. He was not finding this easy. "What is particularly baffling is that the surface of the concrete – such as here," and he pointed to one of the samples, "the surface is relatively unaffected by heat. It leads us to the conclusion, Mr Conrad, that your piece of concrete, and these others, have been subjected to an intense heat not from the outside, but from within the concrete itself."

"How do you explain that?" asked Paul.

"That, of course, is just the point. It is utterly inexplicable. None of us, here or in any university Engineering department, have ever seen anything like it. And believe me, we have seen a lot of concrete that has been subjected to high temperatures – we have samples from nuclear reactors, from Chernobyl and Three Mile Island, from tunnels in which trains of fuel oil have caught fire, and from Cape Canaveral rocket launch pads. Nothing comes even close to explaining what has happened to this. And what we're talking about is a Victorian concrete villa. Frankly, Mr Conrad, if I weren't looking at this with my own eyes, I would say it is completely beyond the laws of what is possible."

"And the concrete survived the heat," said Paul.

"And that's another thing," continued Pollack. "The forces released by the sudden heating, to say nothing of the change of state of the iron, would have been colossal. Easily enough to have blown the concrete apart. And yet that seems not to have happened: you say the house stood until the nineteen-fifties?"

"Yes," replied Paul, "And even then they had to resort to high explosives to demolish it. You don't suppose that could be the explanation?"

"Not a chance. This is off the scale of anything we've ever seen. H.E. could never cause this sort of damage."

Paul took his leave of Desmond Pollack, and his journey home was filled with more questions than answers. If the trauma to the concrete could not be explained by the laws of physics, what other agent could have been at work?

In Duke Humfrey's Library

It was many years since either Paul or Caroline had set foot in the Bodleian library, but the familiar smells immediately brought back memories for both of them: Paul from the years he had spent at Oxford as a postgraduate, and Caroline from hers as a rare book librarian. Martin Prosser, the Keeper of Rare Books and Manuscripts, led them to a vacant table under the richly decorated medieval ceiling of Duke Humfrey's library.

"So remind me what your interest in Massingham is," he said, as they settled down by a window overlooking the Fellows' Garden of Exeter College. The slanting sunlight of the late afternoon caught the leaves on the chestnut trees and reflected off the polished table on which the book in question was laid. It was large – a folio, bound in calf with gilt ornamentation on the cover and spine.

"We're after some information about the Roman temple near Weyford," said Paul, hoping that he would not have to divulge the circumstances of its destruction. "We understand that Massingham describes it in great detail, and that you have the best copy of his book."

"Well, that last bit is certainly true. Our copy was hand-tinted at the time of printing under Massingham's supervision. So we can be pretty certain that the images are very close to what he would have seen on his site visits." Prosser opened the cover with care and laid the book against a foam rest to protect its hinges. The title page announced the volume's scope and intention: *The Roman Antiquities of Surrey, Depicted, Delineated and Described by Ambrose Massingham DD, Antiquary. With forty copper plates, neatly engraved, with an explanation of each plate.* And then the date, MDCCLX. On the subsequent three pages was a list of subscribers to the edition, and a contents list of the sites included.

The book was nothing short of spectacular. The thick handmade paper crackled as the pages turned, each imprinted with large Caslon type, capitalised, italicised, kerned and spaced according to the custom of the day. The plates were separated from the text by thin sheets of tissue to prevent the type from offsetting onto the artwork. Each plate seemed to outdo the last, and Martin Prosser turned them until they revealed the object of the quest: The Temple of Juno near Weyford.

Although Paul and Caroline were familiar with books of the period and knew how impressive they could be, nothing prepared them for the images of the temple remains that greeted them in the series of plates that accompanied the text description. Here was the floor plan, with detailed drawings of the footings to the columns and the few remaining steps that had once led to the door. The next plate showed the caps of some columns, intricately carved and decorated with acanthus leaves. At the next, they gasped in amazement. It showed the mosaic floor with the image of the goddess in the centre. She was dressed in dazzling blues and gold, at her side a peacock, its body bright blue and green, displaying the full glory of its tail feathers.

"It's absolutely astonishing. And the colours are as bright as the day they were painted," said Caroline.

Paul read from the text on the opposite page.

"There are the remains of great pillars of stone and other fragments of this ancient temple, but the most considerable remnant is that of the central mosaic, depicting the goddess Juno: it is among the finest I have ever seen. The parts are so closely joined that it resembles more a continuous picture than an assembly of fragments. The whole is set against a landskip formed from the natural colours of marble. The central figure's gown is of what the Italians call *Smalti*, comprising little pieces of clay, some painted blue and some gilded, all half vitrified. These set off the deity to majestick and most pleasing advantage. She is accompanied by a peacock, which proudly faces the observer with legs straddled and tail feathers fanned. The bird is worked in the most intricate patterns of blue and green glass tesserae. In the upper right corner is depicted the face of a Fury, wreathed in serpents."

The image of the Fury in the plate was of a grotesque gnarled face with coiled snakes for hair. But in the text opposite, the words 'a Fury' had been crossed out and a word written above them in blue-black ink that had smudged slightly. It was a name that sent a chill down the spines of the two researchers. Caroline spoke it out loud.

"Alecto."

"Someone knew their *Aeneid*," said Martin Prosser. "Book Seven, if I remember rightly. Juno rouses her to stir up trouble for the Trojans."

There was a short silence.

"What happened to this bit, I wonder?" said Paul, pointing to the top left-hand corner of the mosaic. A section of the image was missing with only a few tesserae still in place. He continued reading from the text.

"It is much to be regretted that the damage done to the image in earlier times, perhaps by a farmer's plough, has resulted in the loss of an entire corner. It is not known what was therein depicted, but there is reason to believe that there may have been a second face, matching that on the other side."

Paul turned the page back to the chapter heading and the start of the description. His eye was caught by some more textual annotation in the same hand and ink. In the first paragraph the name of the goddess Juno had been underlined, and in the margin of the page was written a short sentence, also underlined. He read out the words.

"Only she can make it stop."

"'Only she can make it stop.' Do you have any idea

what that means?" asked Martin Prosser. Paul and Caroline exchanged glances, neither knowing what to say. Both had the same thought: if the fragment of verse told the story of the villa, whoever wrote those words had no need to have read the *Aeneid*. More probably, the words inked into the folio came from first-hand experience of the goddess and her fiendish Fury.

"Do you know who owned this copy?" Caroline asked, avoiding his question.

"There's a bookplate at the front." He turned to the marbled endpaper, on which was pasted a bookplate: a finely engraved armorial shield, and in a scroll underneath, a Latin motto, *Spero meliora*. Below that, in cursive type, was printed the name Melhuish. "Does that mean anything to you?"

"No, nothing. Apart from the motto, of course. 'I hope for better things'," said Caroline.

Prosser turned a few pages forward and found the name in the list of subscribers: Viscount Melhuish. "I don't know anything about the family I'm afraid," he said.

"How did the Bodleian acquire the book?" asked Paul.

"I'd have to look back at the records. I think we bought it towards the end of the nineteenth century."

"We'd be grateful if you could find out some more," said Paul.

"Can you do copies of these pages for us?" asked Caroline.

"We can." Martin Prosser began to put away the wedges and props that he had used to display the book. "There's an online form, or you can fill a paper one out before you go."

Paul and Caroline thanked the librarian and made their way down the creaking wooden stairs. At the requisition desk they filled in the form for digital imaging. This would take a week or two, they were told, and they would be sent a link to download the files from the internet. In the meantime, there was much work to be done and many leads to follow up.

Paul and Caroline walked down George Street towards the station. Their conversation was restricted to small talk about the viewing of the book, neither wanting to be the first to articulate their true response to the implications of what they had seen. Both felt the ground under their feet to be shifting: what had started as a straightforward matter of historical enquiry had turned into something much bigger. There seemed to be no defined boundaries, and none of the conventional rules seemed to apply. And underlying everything was a growing sense of disquiet that both felt: the past was becoming increasingly and disturbingly mixed up with the present in ways that defied explanation.

For Paul, it was personal. He could not believe that his great-grandfather and his workmen acted deliberately or knowingly in their destruction of the temple remains, but he was now in little doubt that, as a result of their carelessness, powerful forces had been released – forces that were still active, and becoming increasingly threatening. What would come of it next?

Caroline's thoughts were focused on the annotations in the margins of the text they had just seen: the hurried writing, the underlining and the smudged ink suggested that whoever made them was in a state of some turmoil. But who? And how did they come by the book? 'Only she can make it stop.' What did those words mean to the writer? And what did they mean for those who were caught up in it now? For the present, however, these thoughts remained unexpressed.

"There's a train in ten minutes. It gets into Paddington in an hour."

"That's good. Just time to get a coffee." Caroline made her way to the café on the concourse.

They boarded the train, settled into a pair of window seats, and stared at the Oxfordshire landscape speeding past them.

—❧❧—

"So you look at the Melhuish connection, and I'll try to find out more about the sale." Caroline sat at her desk and turned on her computer. It seemed a neat division of labour, but after an hour searching online book auction records and sale catalogues, she was no further forward. Copies of Massingham were scarce and appeared only very rarely in the sale records. And anyway, how did such a fine copy come to be sold from the library of a Viscount?

Paul had no difficulty in tracking down the Melhuish family: the first Viscountcy was created in 1721 for Sir George Melhuish, who had served as an MP and later made a tidy fortune in the East India Company, with which he built a fine Queen Anne style residence to the south west of Weyford. There the family remained until the early 1950s when, unable to meet the demands of death duties, they conveyed it into the care of the National Trust. Paul could find no mention of the disposal of a library – indeed the house's website proclaimed proudly that most of the original furniture and fittings were included in the transfer to the Trust. Beyond that, there was little to go on.

Both strands of research were given a boost by the arrival of an email from Martin Prosser. 'I can confirm that the Bodleian acquired the volume in 1871 from the Weyford antiquarian bookseller Charles Traynor. It would appear to be one of several bought out of the sale of 'the library of a gentleman'. Beyond that I am afraid I am unable to help.'

It was enough.

"1871. The year the Maddox family left Ferndown," Paul said.

"But why would Henry Maddox have a book belonging to Viscount Melhuish? It just doesn't make sense." Caroline's scepticism was hard to refute.

"All right. You see if you can find out about that sale – maybe Charles Traynor still have a copy of the catalogue. And I'll do some digging around Maddox."

Again, Caroline was to be frustrated in her search. A telephone conversation with the bookshop, still trading from its elegant Georgian premises in Mill Street, confirmed the details of the sale, but even at a distance of a hundred and fifty years 'client confidentiality' precluded them from revealing the seller's name. However, Caroline was welcome to consult the copy of the catalogue in the company's archive when next she was in Weyford.

Paul called up a genealogy website and set to work. Henry Maddox was an unusual enough name to make a search reasonably straightforward. Lived in ... Weyford. Married ... whom? Died ... when?

Of ten records returned, two looked promising. 'England and Wales, Civil Registration Marriage Index, 1837-1915. 1849, First Quarter. Maddox, Henry Gilbert,

Weyford.' And then the corresponding entry for the spouse: 'Melhuish, Sarah Louise.'

What came next was a shock: 'Deaths registered in February 1871.' He scrolled down the image of the register to find the name again: 'Maddox, Henry Gilbert.'

—❧❦—

The death of Henry Maddox might explain the family's departure from Ferndown, but what was the explanation for his death? It was a question to which Caroline returned after their summer holiday. Surely such an unexpected event would have been covered in the local newspapers. The online archive returned several results which made for melancholy reading. The *Surrey Messenger* ran a full column.

'The funeral of Mr Henry Maddox, until recently Master Brewer of the firm of Priory Ales, took place yesterday at Holy Trinity Church Weyford. News of his sudden death was received with profound sadness in the town, for he was a much-loved and respected member of the community who will be sadly missed. For some months Mr Maddox had been incapacitated by an affliction of the mind which is believed to have contributed to the fit of apoplexy which he suffered while departing his Weyford villa *en route* for Plymouth, where the family were hoping for his full recovery.

Long before the appointed hour of the funeral, the High Street was crowded with people who had come to pay a last mark of respect to one who had been so great a benefactor to the surrounding district. A large number of people travelled from his native Yorkshire and other places, and the various trains arriving at Weyford station were met by carriages which conveyed the sorrowing mourners to the church.'

Caroline downloaded the cutting and turned to another event, the sale of Ferndown in 1911. Would that too have made the news? She entered some search terms, and again several results were returned. They were even more surprising: 'Severe thunderstorm halts house sale'; 'The thunderstorm over Weyford. Violent electrical storm hits region'; 'Child missing after fearful whirlwind strikes house.'

'The environs of Weyford were struck by a thunderstorm of the utmost ferocity on Thursday last. Hailstones of unprecedented size were recorded, and lightning such as is rarely, if ever, seen in this country struck the North Downs. The event coincided most unfortunately with the sale of a local villa named Ferndown, which was attended by many people. During the sale the house received a most savage lightning strike. The day's proceedings were immediately suspended. Shortly afterwards, a violent whirlwind or tornado was seen to be advancing on the property. A young girl, believed to be the daughter of the villa's owners, was caught in the maelstrom and, despite a thorough search, is still missing. The villa was badly damaged in the storm, and the sale of the property has been called off pending a structural investigation.'

Caroline stared at the cutting. Could this be the reason for the abandonment of the house? What of the little girl, was she ever found? And what happened to the rest of the family? Every piece of information about the house that she turned up seemed to pose further, and more difficult, questions. And through them all there was a constant thread: whoever lived at Ferndown suffered extreme distress of one kind or another and either died or left in unhappy circumstances.

"It all seems to be too much of a coincidence," she said to Paul.

"It does at least offer some explanation as to why the house was never lived in after 1911."

"So we've got an answer to the question we started out with."

"But what about the film? What's that telling us? Why does Juno appear in our copy?"

"Paul, I'll tell you what I think. We should let it go. We've established that this was a house where, for whatever reason, bad things happened. But it was all in the past. It's time to move on now."

"But there are still so many things that we haven't got to the bottom of," said Paul.

"And maybe we should leave them. All we'll do is turn up more unhappiness. There's nothing left of the house now. It's over. Let's find something different to work on. What about that hotel your great-grandfather built in the Scottish Borders?"

"Do you really feel that strongly about it?"

"I do."

"OK then. We'll let it go."

"Good."

There the matter might have rested. Two weeks later, however, a letter arrived which was to change everything.

The Sales Agent

"Some post for you." Caroline sorted the contents of the mailbox into his, hers and junk, and dropped the first pile onto Paul's desk. "There's one from Weyford."

Paul looked at the handwritten envelope and sliced it open with a paperknife. "That handwriting looks familiar," he said, and then, "Yes, it's from Julia Fielding." The letter enclosed a newspaper cutting. He read the letter aloud.

"Dear Mr Conrad, I do hope you don't mind my sending you this, but I've been thinking about the old house ever since you borrowed my father's film. I thought the enclosed story from the *Surrey Messenger* might interest you. It's a bit spooky too, and it mentions a Ferndown Crescent, but I don't suppose there's any connection!"

Caroline picked up the cutting. "Mysterious Death of Law Lecturer," she read. "A fifty-five year old Law lecturer at Weyford College of Law died of a bite from a highly venomous snake. An inquest into the death of Rosemary Nugent of 13, Ferndown Crescent, Weyford, heard that on October 10th she was discovered at a bus stop near the entrance to the college by a colleague, Peter Fleming. Mr Fleming told the inquest that he became concerned when she did not return his greeting. On investigating further, he found her to be unresponsive and called for an ambulance. Paramedics determined that the woman, who was in a seated position at the bus stop, had died. Subsequent tests revealed that she had been dead for approximately an hour before the discovery of her body."

"Ferndown Crescent – that has to be near where the villa used to be," said Paul.

"Very possibly, but this is interesting." Caroline continued reading, "A post-mortem established that the cause of death was a bite to the neck from a tropical snake, probably an Egyptian cobra. An extensive search discovered no sign of a snake at the scene, and it is not known how or why Mrs Nugent came to be at the bus stop. Her car, which she normally used to travel to work, was parked at her home and found to be in perfect working order."

"So how did she come to be bitten by a snake?"

"It doesn't say. The coroner recorded an open verdict and said it was one of the strangest cases she had ever come across."

Paul turned to his computer. "Yes. It's part of the new estate on the site of the villa." He clicked on a link. "At Ferndown Estate choose from a selection of luxurious three- and four-bedroom homes, set in a landscaped development with stunning views across Surrey and beyond and less than an hour's train commute to London. Call our sales team to book an appointment to view."

"So that's what it looks like now. They went up quickly, didn't they?" Caroline looked at the pictures of the new estate, the houses jostling shoulder-to-shoulder where once stood Ferndown, the concrete villa. "How on earth did an Egyptian cobra bite her? And she's found sitting at a bus stop, stone dead. None of it adds up."

Paul turned back to his computer. "According to the site plan, Number Thirteen is this one here," and he pointed to a corner plot near the entrance to the estate. "I'd better drop Julia Fielding a thank-you note. And we need to get the film back to her – she said to hang on to it rather than put it in the post. And maybe before that we could have a look at the new houses? I could 'book an appointment to view.'"

"Paul, we agreed we'd let it go," said Caroline.

"We'll make this our last visit. I promise."

Caroline was still doubtful. "Well, I don't suppose there's any harm in it," she said.

The Ferndown site was almost unrecognisable from Paul and Caroline's previous visits. A new access road had been built, taking a slice off the gardens of two existing houses, and from it smaller cul-de-sacs fanned out in a series of loops and curves to serve the thirteen new houses. Separated by low-growing hedges, each had its own small plot of garden and space for a car in front. Stylistically the houses exhibited a mix of traditional brickwork, dark timber cladding, and white stucco above bargate stone. The larger houses had a garage with a pitched roof. There could hardly have been a starker contrast with the single Italianate villa that had once stood in their place; still less with the classical temple that pre-dated them all by two millennia. A signboard beneath the development company's flag announced that nearly all had been sold: One Home Remaining! View by Appointment Only.

They parked in a space reserved for visitors and took a short walk round the estate. The site was level, the massive concrete retaining wall to the Ferndown terrace having been replaced with a similar one in brick. A tarmac path wound down towards the lower, sloping part of the site which had been left wild.

"We were so lucky to see the place before all this was done. If we'd come even a few weeks later, it would all have gone." Caroline took a photograph from the same vantage point as some of her earlier shots. They would make an interesting contrast.

Paul looked at his watch. "We'd better get up to the show house." They climbed the steps which led up to the end of one of the roadways.

"Remember not to mention what we know about the place. We're here as interested potential purchasers. We've retired, and we're looking for a smaller place with less garden to manage. And we've only recently started thinking about moving." Caroline feared that Paul was quite likely to make an unguarded remark that could give the game away.

"I've learned the script off pat. And watch out for Egyptian cobras."

They passed Number Thirteen, once home to the recently deceased Rosemary Nugent. The curtains on the ground floor were drawn closed, and the grass of the small front lawn was in need of mowing. Next to it was their destination, the show house: its purpose fulfilled, it too was now being sold. Caroline rang the bell, and some few seconds later the door was opened.

"How nice to meet you. I'm Alexis. Do come in and have a look round, and then we can talk." The practiced charm of the sales agent was matched by her tidy, well-groomed appearance: a figure-hugging two-piece suit, the skirt demurely knee-length; sensible shoes with a low heel; a white blouse open at the collar revealing a flash of a gold necklace. Her dark hair framed an oval face which wore little make-up. The professional appearance was finished off with a red folder clutched in her left hand, leaving the right free to shake hands with her clients.

"Thank you. We've been walking round the estate. It looks very nice." Paul stood aside to let Caroline accompany Alexis into the house. The tour took in the open plan dining room and kitchen, the living room "with this sizeable conservatory – it's lovely in the summer, and the thermal glass we use will keep it warm in the winter;" upstairs the four bedrooms, one with en-suite, "and you must look at the view from the master bedroom." After a while Alexis said, "I'll let you look round on your own, and then we can get together downstairs." Paul and Caroline drifted around the house long enough to show convincing purpose, after which Paul descended the two steps from the conservatory into the garden while Caroline made a more detailed inspection of the kitchen. They reconvened in the living room and settled awkwardly into armchairs that were slightly too small for comfort.

"So, do you have a property to sell, or could you make an immediate purchase?"

"We're still on the market, but we've had some very positive interest." Paul knew that his response would lose him credibility as a serious purchaser. These days most people had their finance in place before they set foot in a new property. After some more discussion in the same vein Caroline took the opportunity to make a move. "We ought to be getting on, we've another appointment shortly."

The studied politeness continued as they stepped into the driveway. "Thank you so much for your interest. My contact details are in the information pack. I hope I'll hear from you again."

"I hope so too – it's just the sort of place we're looking for, and such a lovely spot," said Paul.

"Yes. Though it's changed a bit since you were last here."

Paul and Caroline both stiffened, each suppressing an urge to kick the other. Their looks spoke their feelings. I thought we agreed not to talk about it. You said you knew the script off pat.

"Goodbye, and thank you for showing us round."

Alexis watched as they got into the car and allowed herself a smile as she observed the unhappy little scene that played out before they drove off. It was a start. Soon she would begin in earnest.

The distance between Ferndown and Julia Fielding's house was short, and even in busy traffic took no more than half an hour. But in that space of time, everything changed. The issue of who had let on to Alexis that they had an interest in the site beyond a house viewing was swiftly despatched: neither had said a word, and anyway it was a trivial matter. What was more puzzling was how Alexis had known of their previous visit, and why she had chosen to mention it. Then, on that last visit, the concrete retaining wall of the old villa's terrace was still standing, and the thirteen houses of the new estate were no more than drawings on a plan. And the only people they had met had been the team of archaeologists, hardly a likely channel of information to the young sales agent. As Paul drove slowly up the steep hills of the North Downs town, Caroline flicked through the brochure that Alexis had given them. She picked up a business card, and read her name: 'Alexis Tobin, Sales Executive for Greenlea Homes.' Alexis Tobin.

"Alexis Tobin," she said. "That's her name. The sales agent."

"I don't suppose we'll hear from her again. Didn't she say that she had three other viewings today? I'm sure in her eyes we barely qualify as prospective purchasers."

Caroline did not reply. In her mind's eye she was imagining the picture of the Roman mosaic in the book; Juno, the goddess with the peacock; and the head of the Fury with snakes for hair. Alecto. No, surely it was just a coincidence. And what about the death of the Law lecturer? From a snake bite. From an Egyptian cobra for heaven's sake. Alexis Tobin. It's changed a bit since you were last here. Alecto. Alice. Here is no abiding stay. None shall here inherit. Juno. Only she can make it stop.

"Paul. Stop the car. Pull over for a minute."

Paul parked in a layby and looked at Caroline. He could read the fear in her eyes. Her breathing was fast, and the emotion broke her speech into short, clipped sentences.

"I want to try to get a few things straight. Before we

go to Julia Fielding's. And please don't tell me I'm being silly. It's stopped being a game. Someone's died. And I think somehow she's behind it."

"Julia Fielding?"

"No. Alexis Tobin. Alecto."

The Fragment Decoded

"Well, I nearly said when I opened the door that you looked as if you'd seen a ghost. And now you tell me that you think you just have!" Julia Fielding's laughter came as a welcome relief, a gentle reminder of the world as it should be, as it used to be, before "all this stuff" as Paul called it, began. Warmed and cheered by tea and cake, he and Caroline recounted the events of the past few months. At first their narrative was disjointed and hesitant, but as it became clear that Julia took their findings seriously, both felt more able to express thoughts that until now they had not even shared with each other. Gradually, and with some prompting from their host, the couple's story fell into place.

"How extraordinary about the Latin graffiti on the wall. And the poem could have been written about the villa, couldn't it?" Julia read the description of the atrium: "'The gilded stair, the mirror, doubling the insult in its reflecting pane,' and it even gets the words round the gallery right too, doesn't it? 'Commodity, firmness and delight'. Is there any way that the architect could have read it, do you think?"

"I suppose it's possible," said Paul, "but there's so much more in it that fits, too: the way the ruins of the temple are destroyed, and the description of the mosaic floor – which matches the description in the book – and then of course there's all the stuff about Alecto."

Caroline continued Paul's train of thought: "You mentioned last time that when you saw the apparition of the little girl, – if that's what it was – you heard her say something about Alice not being really called Alice."

"Yes that's right. She said that her real name was Electra."

"You don't think what you heard as Electra could have been Alecto?"

"It could have been, I suppose, but I couldn't say for sure. It was nearly sixty years ago. Did you say that you found out something about Lucy?"

"Yes. We did some work on the last family to live in the house, some people called Ramsden. They had a daughter who we think must have been killed in the lightning strike." Caroline turned some pages in the file of research, but Julia motioned her to stop.

"Maybe the best thing would be to try to do a summary from the start. I'm getting confused with all the people living there."

Paul took the lead. "You could say it starts in AD forty-something, when the fragment of poetry was written. Everything that happens after that is just a working-out of the goddess's curse. But if we take the earliest facts we know, we're looking at about 1870, when Henry Maddox commissions William Westmacott to design a villa. Maddox is the Master Brewer of Priory Ales in Weyford. He's from the north, but his wife is from Weyford; she's from a well-to-do family, the Melhuishes. They used to live at Bramford Park."

"And the architect decides to build the villa in concrete, which is where your great-grandfather comes in," said Julia.

"Either the architect decides, or Henry Maddox persuades him. Maddox was very keen on using the latest ideas in everything. Either way, it makes no difference."

"But it all starts to go wrong when the builders dig up the remains of the temple and make concrete with it?"

"That's what the poem says. And we do know from the analysis of the concrete that it definitely had bits of Roman mosaic and brick mixed up in it."

"What makes you think that the Maddox family were affected by Juno's curse?" asked Julia.

"It's only circumstantial evidence," said Caroline. "First, Henry Maddox dies in 1871. The death certificate suggests that he was of unsound mind, but the actual cause of death seems to have been some sort of seizure. The other bit of evidence is in the book that the archaeologist referred us to: Massingham's *Roman Antiquities of Surrey*. It's a huge eighteenth-century volume, with lovely illustrations. It describes the ruins of the temple as they were before Charles Partridge's builders got at them. The copy we looked at in the Bodleian has the Melhuish family bookplate on the endpaper; and in the description of the temple, against a mention of a Fury, someone has written the name Alecto and, where it refers to Juno, there's a strange sentence in the same writing which says, 'Only she can make it stop'."

"We think it must it have been Maddox who wrote that," said Paul.

"Couldn't it have been written later?" asked Julia.

"The library at Ferndown was sold in 1871, and that's when the Bodleian bought their copy. As far as we know, it's only ever been in the Melhuish family, and it's sold out of Maddox's library. So there's a strong possibility that it must have been either Maddox or his wife who made the annotations."

"And what do you think the 'it' is that only Juno can stop?"

Paul picked up the copy of the fragment of poetry. "We don't know, of course, but if we assume that Alecto is at work on Juno's instructions, then she's bringing 'nightmares, torment and despair' to anyone who lives there and making sure that no-one inherits the place. Which is what happens."

"It's quite a leap of the imagination to say that's why Henry Maddox died," said Julia Fielding.

"I think the poem is the key to understanding it." Caroline took the sheet of paper from Paul. "There are two things here that upset Juno. The first is seeing her image being ground up by the stone crusher and put in the cement mixer. That's what this bit about 'the ghastly engines' is all about. It says, she feels the wounds 'as if inflicted on her person.'"

"And the second?" Julia prompted.

"That's more about her vanity. It took us a while to work this out, but we think we know what's going on. Juno goes into the house and sees the precepts of Vitruvius, 'commodity, firmness and delight', written around the gallery. That's bad enough, but it's what happens next that really gets her. The 'ancient grievance' is a reference to the Judgment of Paris, which was a beauty contest between three goddesses. Paris declares Venus to be more beautiful than Juno or Minerva. Juno is furious at being judged second best."

Paul continued the story. "In the fragment, Juno enters the villa and sees a statue of Venus standing in the big hall, and that's what incenses her. Well, we discovered that Henry Maddox did install a statue of Venus in the great hall of Ferndown. So, quite unwittingly, he has delivered the greatest insult imaginable to Juno. He's destroyed her image in the temple, mixed it into the fabric of his villa, written words that taunt her around the walls, and put a statue of her greatest rival in the atrium."

"And if there's one goddess you wouldn't want to

get on the wrong side of, it's Juno," said Caroline. She can bear a grudge like no other."

"This is what she says about it," said Paul, reading from the fragment:

> "'I have
> endured enough. No greater outrage could be committed here.
> Venus shall not remain within these walls, and he
> who set her here shall rue the day!" With that
> she calls Alecto from her hellish den to do her bidding.'

Henry Maddox doesn't stand a chance against that. He probably never realises what he's done, but from the moment he moves into Ferndown, he's toast."

Julia Fielding laughed. "So let's assume that's Henry Maddox taken care of, then. Who lived there next?"

"There are several families in the census returns after 1871, but we started at the other end, with the people who lived there last," said Caroline. "They were a family called Ramsden. He worked in the Stock Exchange, and they had three children, two boys and a girl."

"And the girl is called Lucy?"

"That's right. She was born in 1901."

"And what happens to them?"

"We haven't yet found any record of them after they leave Ferndown in 1911. And strangely we can't find a birth or a death certificate for Lucy. It's all still a mystery."

"Is there anything that suggests why they left Ferndown?"

"Again, not directly," said Paul. "But this is where the concrete research comes in. We had some of it analysed by the Concrete Foundation, and they discovered that it had been subjected to extraordinarily high temperatures. It was hot enough not just to melt the iron reinforcement that the builders put in it but to completely vaporise it. They were unable to explain how that could have happened."

"But you can." Julia smiled at Paul encouragingly.

"We can't explain what happened, but we do think we know when it did. The Ramsdens had decided to sell up in 1911 – there's a catalogue of the sale of the house and contents in the History Centre. But on the day of the sale there was the most terrific thunderstorm. Caroline found several references to it in the papers. The *Surrey Messenger* carried a report saying that Ferndown was struck by lightning, and a lot of structural damage was done. And there's mention of the Ramsdens' daughter Lucy being missing after the storm, and as Caroline said, we haven't been able to find an entry for her death."

"Maybe Juno threw a thunderbolt at the villa," said Julia, and they laughed.

"There's an academic paper about the storm," said Caroline. "It was what's called a supercell – where lots of thunderstorms combine to form one big one. They don't happen very often. At least, not in Surrey."

"And the other thing that the paper reports is that

Lucy saved many people's lives by running into the house and shouting a warning right before the lightning strike," said Paul.

"How would she know what was about to happen?" asked Julia.

"We don't know," said Paul, "But you could argue that it sets a precedent for her appearance to you, warning you about Alice."

"What have you found out about the house after the Ramsdens left?"

"In the History Centre there's a typescript article written by a local historian. Like you, he says it was used as a chicken farm between the wars, so presumably it was uninhabitable after the storm damage. After that, the next reference is to the demolition in the nineteen-fifties. Which brings us to your father's film." Paul paused. He had not yet told Julia of the apparition that had superimposed itself on the digital copy, but now the time felt right. "When we digitised the film, there was something strange about the copy we made."

"Go on. I'm all ears."

"I'm not making this up. And the chap who did the transfer saw it too. We saw the figure of a woman dressed in blue, walking into the house before the explosion. And she was still there, on the terrace, after the dust settled. With a peacock. It wasn't on the film – only on the copy."

"Juno?"

"That's what we thought."

Paul opened his laptop and ran the digitised copy.

"That's quite extraordinary.   I certainly don't remember seeing her before," said Julia. "So, what you're telling me is, two thousand years after that bit of poetry was written, she's still angry, and she's got it in for anyone who buys the villa, is that right?"

Caroline shifted uneasily, collecting her thoughts. "It would be nice if that's all it was, but I think there's more to it than that. The villa has gone now, and the last remaining vestige of it, the retaining wall to the terrace, has also been broken up. So you might expect that the supernatural activity, whatever it is, might have stopped too. In fact we assumed that it had until we got your letter."

"With the cutting from the *Messenger*," said Julia. "What a horrible thing to happen to that poor woman. Can you imagine?"

"We think it's still going on. And she's the latest victim," said Caroline.

"And quite possibly not the last." Paul's voice was quiet, as if he were speaking to himself.

"Why do you think that?"

"It may be a coincidence, but the activity seems to peak whenever the concrete is disturbed," said Paul. "The first, obviously, is when the remains of the temple are dug up and crushed into concrete.   Next there's the demolition by the Royal Engineers. The concrete is torn apart by explosives, and on the video the goddess appears with her peacock. And then there's the present day. The chap at the Concrete Foundation said that they went to the site to collect some more samples, and got there just before the builders broke it all up to use as hardcore. Once again, it's been broken into pieces and rammed into a new place. Shortly afterwards we have another unexplained death."

"So you think there's something in the concrete itself?"

"Possibly. It's noticeable that any time it's broken up, or blown up, something nasty happens," said Paul. "It's as if something, or someone, is being woken up."

"And that something or someone is . . . ?"

"Alecto." Caroline picked up the fragment again, and found the lines describing her.

> "'The Fury loathed even by her kin, she who can
> assume the shape of any form, with hair of coiled snakes,
> her visage so grotesque it drives men mad: Alecto,
> now let loose to punish the wrongs of heedless men.'"

"And let's remember that the Law lecturer, Rosemary Nugent, died of a snakebite. It's Alecto's stock-in-trade," said Paul.

"How would she have come into contact with her?" asked Julia Fielding. Caroline took a deep breath. This wasn't going to be easy.

"We, or at least I – I can't answer for Paul because

we've hardly had time to discuss it – I think that she's 'assumed the shape' as the poem has it, of the sales agent for the development company of the new houses on the Ferndown site."

Julia looked at Caroline to see if she was serious. She stifled laughter and then, unable to stop, let it out. "You mean she's come back as an estate agent! That's too wonderful! Not even Virgil could have dreamed that one up!" She stopped, fearing she had overstepped the mark. "I'm sorry, it's just so unexpected!"

"Yes, you could hardly make it up, could you?" Caroline reached for the sales particulars of the house they had visited and expanded on their meeting. "So in effect, she's hiding in plain view. She knows who we are; she knows that we've visited the site; she's even using a name that gives the game away. Alexis Tobin. And crucially she also knows that no-one would ever believe us. Can you imagine going into a police station and telling the desk sergeant that we know how Rosemary Nugent died and that the sales agent is really a Roman Fury with snakes for hair, whose hatred knows no bounds?"

"That I would love to see," said Paul.

"That's why she made the remark about the place having changed since our last visit: she's revealing to us who she is, secure in the knowledge that we can't do anything about it. And she'll probably go through the whole estate with her 'nightmares, torment and despair' act, and no-one will ever suspect her." Caroline was becoming agitated, and Julia sought to calm the mood.

"I'm not saying I don't believe you. You've presented me with such an extraordinary story that I honestly don't know what's what any more. What do you make of it, Paul?"

"I think that there must be a way to turn Alecto off. Juno summons her and sets her to work when she says – where is it now? Ah yes,

> 'Come, Daughter of the Night, you of a thousand names
> and deadly guiles, whose hatred knows no bounds!
> Perform this one last labour – do me this service now!'

If it's her one last labour, it should be possible to say 'job done' to her. But as to how . . ."

"I think you may be looking in the wrong place," said Julia Fielding. "What were the words that you found written in the book? 'Only she can make it stop.' That's what Henry Maddox knew, and he may be right. I think you need to go to Juno. Only she can make it stop."

Menù Italiano

"To my way of thinking, either none of it is true, or all of it is. There isn't a middle way." Caroline put down her wine glass, and an attentive waiter refilled it. The Trattoria Romana was a favourite of theirs, and to Paul and Caroline it seemed an appropriate venue to discuss the way forward. The restaurant was on the first floor of a range of Edwardian buildings leading off Leicester Square, and their window table enjoyed a view of the busy street below and the green space of the square beyond.

"OK then, let's assume it's all true: everything we said to Julia Fielding is how it is, and any day now there's going to be another piece of unpleasantness from Alexis, or Alecto," said Paul.

"Followed by another, and another. She doesn't give up. Once she's given a task, she keeps on going. And what worries me is that she obviously knows about us. Who's to say we won't be her next target?"

"That's fairly unlikely, don't you think? So far the only people she's had a go at have actually bought a house on the site – either the villa, or now, it seems, one on the new estate."

Caroline was unconvinced. "So why did she go to the trouble of making it very clear that she knows who we are? Maybe she knows that we've worked out what's going on.   Maybe she knows that there's a family connection between you and Charles Partridge.   And I wouldn't mind betting that somehow she's behind the Latin graffiti painted on the wall. She's setting a trap for us, Paul."

There was a pause while the waiter brought their main courses and performed the usual ritual with parmesan and pepper. "Prego. Enjoy your meal."

"Thank you," said Paul, and then, returning to the business in hand, "OK, so what are our options?"

"We could call her bluff. Confront Alexis. Tell her what we know."

"Too risky," replied Paul. "If she really is a shape-shifting demon, she'll throw a couple of her asps in our direction, and we'll be her next victims."

"Supposing we did nothing? Just walked away from the whole thing and got back to what we were doing before all this started?" Caroline knew as she spoke that this was a non-starter.

"And then more people on the Ferndown Estate die. And Julia Fielding says, you knew about this: why didn't you try to stop it?"

"All right then, let's go back to that idea of telling someone in authority. Get it off our chest, and we're in the clear if something bad happens."

"Who would believe us? The only thing we can tell them about the woman who was bitten by the snake is pure supposition. Besides, as you said, that 'something bad' could just happen to us." Paul poured two glasses from a large water bottle. "How's your cannelloni?"

"Very good." Caroline was beginning to run out of ideas. "The only other option is to do as Julia Fielding suggested and go straight to Juno. Remember, 'Only she can make it stop'".

"Or, as Sherlock Holmes said, 'When you have eliminated the impossible, whatever remains, however improbable, must be the truth.'"

"Hm. It's not exactly elementary though, is it? Getting in touch with a Roman goddess."

They ate for a while in silence.

"Of course the Romans took these things very seriously. They wouldn't do anything important without making some sort of offering to the gods," said Paul. "You wouldn't want to offend them."

"What sort of offering?" asked Caroline.

"I don't know. Didn't they sacrifice animals? Sheep, goats, that sort of thing."

"I absolutely draw the line at that, Paul. Positively no blood sacrifices, thank you very much."

The waiter cleared their plates and brought the dessert menu which occupied their attention for the next few minutes. "Chocolate gelato, please," said Caroline; "Tiramisu for me," said Paul, "And a half bottle of Vin Santo, please."

Caroline made another suggestion. "Maybe we could offer up some prayers or something. If we knew where to find her."

"Let's think about that one," said Paul. "What was it that upset her in the first place? In the poem?"

"The destruction of her image in the mosaic, and what was left of her temple."

"Quite. So that's what we need to put right, isn't it? The act of destruction."

"What are you suggesting, Paul?"

"I know what we have to do. And I think I know how we can do it."

"What?"

"We must rebuild the temple."

Caroline looked hard at her husband. "Rebuild the temple. How, exactly?"

"I've got an idea, but I'll need to do some research on it. And there's someone we need to go back to. Do you remember that archaeologist and her students we met the second time we went to Ferndown?"

"Margaret Pearson? How could I forget her? She practically threw us off the site."

"That's her. I have a feeling that she holds the key to the whole thing. But it won't be easy."

PAST AND PRESENT

"Juno. A fascinating figure. She's one of the most complex of all the classical gods – and the queen of them all. She's the goddess of marriage and childbirth – though her own marriage was something of a disaster. Jupiter, her husband, was also her brother and a frightful womaniser. She's a fearless warrior, but she's also associated with fertility. She's vindictive and unforgiving, but at the same time she's a defender and protector, especially of women. There are so many sides to her."

"So, like many women, she's rather good at multi-tasking," said Paul.

Margaret Pearson paused and looked at him. Caroline had succumbed to a cold, leaving Paul to meet the archaeologist on his own. Their first encounter had begun and ended badly; and on this, the second, there was still tension in the air. Her office, in a converted church near Weyford, was cluttered with objects and the rack shelving on each wall housed rows of box files. Paul noticed on her desk the piece of concrete she had demanded on their site visit, and it brought back painful memories.

The archaeologist continued, "Now, you did tell me a little on the telephone, but I don't understand why you are so interested in Juno, when your own line of research is in Victorian concrete."

"It's hard to explain," said Paul, "but ever since you discovered that the concrete villa incorporated the remains of the temple, we've found that they are, quite literally, mixed up together. The villa seems to have been an unhappy place to live – no-one stayed there long, and eventually it was abandoned, only forty years after it was built. At least one person died there in rather mysterious circumstances, and others seem to have been driven mad."

"Are you suggesting that the unhappiness was a result of the destruction of the temple remains?" asked Margaret Pearson.

"Suppose I tell you what we've found, and perhaps you can then tell me what you think," said Paul, and he outlined their findings just as he had for Julia Fielding the week before, culminating in the death of the Law lecturer.

"So to summarise, and this must sound completely ridiculous, we believe that the Ancient Romans are still somehow having an influence on us today," Paul concluded. Margaret Pearson sat silently, marshalling her thoughts.

"Mr Conrad, I am a scientist. I've been trained in archaeological techniques, and over the years I have amassed a certain amount of knowledge. The subject matter of my work, the remains, the artefacts, and the habitations of ancient people, are the products of belief systems that underpinned their very existence. I have worked all over the world, from Maori and Aboriginal sites to the sacred places of Native Americans, and again and again I have come across instances where our own forefathers, by their disrespectful behaviour towards those people, have created problems for us now: their descendants are still resentful. Whether it's the relic-hunting that the Victorians seemed to have a passion for, or the clash of cultures that we still see today in some countries, the result is the same. That's why, increasingly, we archaeologists have to question everything we do when we explore ancient sites, and why we now have to spend so much time debating what to do about the situations we have inherited from our predecessors."

"But in this instance, no indigenous people are involved, and wholly innocent people, like Rosemary Nugent, are suffering – if our inferences are correct, of course," said Paul.

"I would expect that all of the things you told me about the villa could be explained perfectly rationally. It is only when you put them together that they appear to acquire a supernatural dimension, and then simply by," and she paused to find the right words, "by accretion and association."

"Do you think buildings can hold the memory of things that happened in them – or to them?" Paul pressed her.

"I'm not the right person to ask. Of course, there are people who give credence to such ideas, but as a scientist, I can deal only in things which can be observed and measured. And if you are asking me whether I believe in the power of ancient curses, I would have to say no, I don't, and I have never come across any instance of anyone being affected by one. But I will acknowledge that things done in the past can have implications for us in the present, and we can sometimes do something about that."

"Let's say then, that my great-grandfather is one of those Victorians you referred to, who was disrespectful to an ancient place – though we don't know whether he was even aware of the existence of the temple. Is there anything we can do about it now?"

"When you telephoned me, I think you said you had something in mind," Margaret Pearson looked at Paul expectantly.

"Dr Pearson, I do believe that the destruction of the temple ruins by my great-grandfather is somehow behind the unhappiness that has befallen the people who have lived there afterwards. I also think that we can do something about it. I believe that the best way to make amends is to rebuild the temple. Not physically of course. Not in bricks and mortar. In virtual reality. On a computer."

Margaret Pearson had not expected such an original proposal.

"And what would be the point of that?"

"If the Ancient Romans offended a god, they would make an offering. As I understand it, that usually involved slaughtering a cow or some other animal. I'm not up for that, but this would be, as it were, my offering, from the present to the past, to try to put things right."

"Mr Conrad, as far as I know, you don't believe in Juno. You knew next to nothing about her until recently. Are you sure you aren't just trying to expiate your own feelings of guilt for your great-grandfather's mistake?"

Paul considered Margaret Pearson's stricture.

"Well, maybe I am. And I agree that the evidence for the existence of a curse is circumstantial. But you haven't explained the coincidence of the fragment of poetry, or how a quotation from it found its way onto the terrace wall of the villa. I still think there's more to it."

"You will need to show me some real evidence rather than vague coincidences."

"May I show you the film that I referred to?" said Paul, reaching for his laptop, "With Juno in the tower room."

Margaret Pearson indicated her consent. Paul moved the file and the concrete on her desk and angled the laptop screen so they both could see it.

"What you'll see is, before the explosion she walks across the front of the building, enters it, and then appears in a room at the top of the tower. After the demolition she's outside again, looking straight at the camera. You can even hear a peacock on the sound track." As he spoke, the first frame of the film appeared on the screen, and they sat back to watch.

Once again the long shot before the explosion ran, with the call to 'Take Cover!' But this time there was no sign of the Lady in Blue. The order 'Fire!' was given, and the building erupted in the ensuing explosion. And once again, the dust settled and the soldiers carried out their inspection but with no sign of the figure in the foreground. Paul stopped the playback.

"I can assure you that she was there when I saw this with the film editor. There was no doubt whatsoever," Paul said, mystified. "And she was there when Caroline saw it too."

"I think we may need to agree to differ on your supernatural interpretation," said Margaret Pearson. "Recreating the temple in VR is an idea that interests me, though. As I said the last time we met, the destruction of the mosaic is an incalculable loss. It is true that we have a good account of it and a particularly fine illustration in Massingham. And we have a fairly clear idea of the structure of the temple – the shape and size, and the materials used. Until recently we relied on scale models to give us an idea of the whole. The techniques we are using now to create an illusion of being actually inside a building are quite remarkable – I don't doubt they will transform our interpretation and understanding of the past."

It took Paul a moment to digest the archaeologist's conclusion. Against his expectations from her earlier remarks, she had not dismissed his idea out of hand.

"So, how could we take this forward?" he asked.

"There's not much I can do; besides I'm semi-retired now. I would suggest you speak to Sandra Thorne. She was part of the team from Cambridge that you met at the site. She knows more about this sort of thing than I do, and she's working for a company that specialises in such reconstructions." She rummaged in a drawer. "Here's her card. Why don't you contact her?"

Paul thanked Margaret Pearson and took his leave of her.

He returned to find Caroline under a blanket on the sofa and recounted the events of the day. "I don't understand that video," he said. "You saw the figure when I brought it home, didn't you?"

"Yes. I can't explain it either," said Caroline. "We must look at it again. And when I'm over this cold, I'd be up for a trip to Cambridge."

Margaret Pearson stayed late at the old church, now home to the Surrey Archaeological Trust. The trouble with amateur historians, she thought, is that they can't see the bigger picture. They come along with half-baked theories that don't stand a moment's scrutiny against the known facts, and they put two and two together and make – goodness knows how much. More than four in the case of the Conrad couple, that was certain.

She looked at the file on the Weyford temple which lay open on her desk. She had not paid any attention to it since her realisation that the last vestiges of the Roman remains had been reconstituted as aggregate for a Victorian villa. The act of destruction still offended her; and as she looked at the plates copied from the Massingham folio, she grieved for the loss of the magnificent mosaic floor. The image of Juno, statuesque, commanding and regal, dominated the frame. The artist had depicted her face to perfection, combining in equal measure her haughtiness and compassion. The tail of the peacock at her side glowed on the page, the hundred eyes on its feathers painted in rich blues and greens. The archaeologist's gaze moved to the vengeful face of the Fury with its snakes for hair, and across to the empty space where its counterpart had once completed the whole. How she would love to see it as it had once been, entire and complete.

The evening light from the west window filled the room which had been carved out of the church by the addition of a mezzanine floor, dividing its space into two levels. Above, the timber roof trusses caught the rays of the setting sun. Margaret Pearson sat with her back to the light and read the poem which Paul Conrad had left on the desk, *The goddess Juno foresees the ruin of her temple*. She had to admit there was a close correlation between the narrative of the fragment and the events on the Weyford site. And what of the deaths? Were they just coincidence too? She closed her eyes. She was being asked to believe too much, to give credence to fanciful supposition. She pondered Paul Conrad's question: Do buildings retain the memory of things that happened in them? She could not refute the idea, though it went against her entire conviction. What of this building, once a church, and now an office and a laboratory? Does its fabric retain a memory of its history? And what of all the sites that she had spent so much time investigating, that were held sacred by the ancients and their descendants? She had no answers, but the questions continued to crowd in on her.

Waking from her reverie, she picked up the piece of concrete salvaged from the temple site, its fabric now uniting ancient and more recent history. The clean face which she had recently cleft revealed tantalising glimpses of the mosaic's tesserae. Massingham must have been the last person to have seen them *in situ*, to record them, to recognise them in their glory. And before him, centuries before him, another civilisation honoured them, made offerings and worshipped in the temple that housed them. She brushed some cement dust off the surface and found another small piece of the glassy clay.

It was a soft pink in colour. She looked across to the picture of the mosaic floor. Was it from the face of Juno? Or from the Fury? Or was it a small fragment from the missing section? It was impossible to say.

The sun by now had set, and the last light of day was fading. Margaret Pearson turned to reach for the light switch. A sound from the corner of the room startled her. It was the sound of a door opening, followed by footsteps on a wooden stair, slow and deliberate. It was an unremarkable sound, save for the fact that there was no-one else in the building and no stair in the direction from which it was coming. The stairs to the new floor were on the other side of the room. Margaret Pearson strained to look into the gathering dark and saw, emerging out of the half-light, the bent figure of an old woman slowly ascending through the solid mezzanine floor. The creature, whatever it was, straightened a little and set course for the desk behind which the archaeologist sat transfixed. As it came closer, she could see the face of the apparition more clearly. It was the same face that was staring out from the page of the Massingham folio: the face of a Fury, wreathed in serpents.

A Window on the World

"It's amazing what they're doing. Almost any building can be recreated in virtual reality – and they can even superimpose missing bits onto existing ones. So if you're in Tintern Abbey, say, you put on the VR glasses and they will show you what it looked like before it was ruined. Apparently you can move around, too, and it still works." Paul Conrad scrolled down the website and read, "'At Fenestra Virtuality we create digital models of vanished worlds. Based on accurate archaeological research, our virtual environment allows you to visit ancient cities, explore them in safety and comfort, and even interact with their inhabitants. Fenestra offers enhanced on-site realisation too. Our digital reconstructions show you buildings and cities as they would have appeared to their original builders. Experience the wonders of the past using the latest 3-D technology,' etc., etc."

"Is that where Sandra Thorne works?" asked Caroline.

"Yes. It says here that she studied archaeology at Cambridge, specialised in rescue archaeology for a few years, then founded this company. They're based just outside Cambridge."

"I think we should get in touch with her."

The two spent the rest of the morning drafting an email to Sandra Thorne which they hoped would say enough about why Fenestra should recreate the Roman temple, without going into detail about the unwelcome visitations from the ancient world into the present. That could wait for later.

In the afternoon they set about organising the files that they would need to take in the event of a visit to Fenestra. Caroline collated the scans they had ordered from the Bodleian Library, while Paul pulled together a dossier to support their reasoning for rebuilding the temple. Their tasks complete, Paul said, "I'll load the files onto my laptop."

"OK. Fancy a cup of tea?"

"Yes, please."

There was silence as they went about their allotted tasks, but as she was making the tea, Caroline heard Paul give a cry of amazement. She ran up the half-flight of stairs to his study. "Whatever is it?" she asked.

Paul was standing in front of his laptop staring at what was on the screen. Caroline recognised it as the last shot of the video.

"Look at this." Paul scrolled back to the point immediately before the soldiers departed after checking the wrecked building for unexploded charges. "This is where I stopped the film when I was with Margaret Pearson," he said. "But look what happens next."

Slowly, and with some difficulty, a figure struggled out from the shattered remains of the villa. Clad in brown, and stooping, it made a short detour round some fallen concrete and turned to walk towards the camera. It became clear from its gait that the figure was that of an old woman. At first her face was obscured by the hood that entirely covered her head. As she came closer, she raised both hands and cast the hood backwards, revealing her face. Both viewers reeled back from the screen. The face of the old woman was drawn and cadaverous, the eyes sunk darkly into her sallow cheeks. And her head was topped, unmistakeably, not with hair, but with thin, coiled, writhing snakes.

"God, it's her!" said Caroline. "It's Alecto!"

The old woman looked directly into the lens, made a grimace accompanied by a low hissing sound, and left the shot as if continuing past the static camera. Then the film ended as before.

"She's on the loose," said Paul. "Where will she turn up next?"

"Paul, I don't like this," said Caroline.

"Neither do I. We have to stop her." He ran the film back a few frames until the image of the old woman appeared, and pressed a key on the laptop.

Caroline started. "What are you doing?"

"I'm going to print a screenshot. We need hard proof that she's part of the film."

He saved the file, turned the printer on, and line by line the screenshot appeared on paper. It was one of the most hideous images imaginable. Paul put the printout in a folder and closed the laptop.

The evening brought another setback in the form of an email reply from Sandra Thorne.

Dear Mr Conrad,

Thank you for your email. I am afraid we will be unable to help you with your proposal to recreate the Weyford Temple of Juno in virtual reality. While it is undoubtedly an interesting and worthwhile project, we have to prioritise our output, and each commission must be accompanied by a costed business plan before we will consider accepting it. At present we are fully engaged on digitising a number of ancient sites that are considered to be at risk, especially those in areas of conflict, and that is another reason why I must decline your request. We do however have long-term plans to create a virtual journey through Roman Britain, and we will certainly consider including the temple in that portfolio when it comes to fruition.

With all good wishes,

Sandra Thorne,

Digital Content Producer, Fenestra Virtuality.

"Well that's that then, I suppose," said Caroline. "Can you think of another way?"

"Not at the moment," replied Paul. "They're the best hope we have of doing VR." Their dejection and disappointment were almost tangible, and the cold rainy evening did little to lift their mood.

Over dinner that night Caroline found a way to brighten their gloom.

"We both need to get away from all this. Why don't we take a city break?"

"That's the best idea I've heard all day," said Paul. "Did you have anywhere in mind?"

"Barcelona."

"Sounds good to me," said Paul.

"Great food, shopping, the museums . . ."

"I've heard there's some rather interesting concrete too," said Paul.

Prime Suspect

The couple's plans for a Spanish holiday were disrupted by a telephone call.

"For you, Paul. Surrey Police."

Caroline listened as Paul took the call.

"Yes, yes I did have a meeting with her. . . It was on Thursday afternoon . . . Er, I left around five. . . Yes, she seemed absolutely fine, nothing wrong at all. . . How dreadful. . . Do you have any idea what happened? . . . I see. . . Yes of course, that would be fine. . . We live in London . . . Yes, that would be no problem, I'll help any way I can. . . No. . . . Goodbye."

Paul put down the phone and turned to Caroline. "Margaret Pearson was found dead yesterday. At the Archaeology Trust, where I met her."

"God, how awful. How did she die, did they tell you?"

"They're not saying, except that they think it's suspicious. They think she's been murdered. And they want to talk to me."

—❧—

"Thank you for coming to talk to us, Mr Conrad. I'm sure that with your help we can clear this up quickly." The detective-sergeant ran through the formalities with Paul, and then the questions began.

"What can you tell me about your movements on the day in question, that is, Thursday, the ninth of March, Mr Conrad?"

"I left London at about half past two and drove to Weyford. I arrived just after a quarter to four. I was early for my meeting with Dr Pearson, so I parked on the forecourt, walked for ten minutes or so, then went in to the Archaeological Trust."

"And when was your meeting arranged for?"

"Four o'clock."

"What was the purpose of your meeting?"

"I hoped to interest Dr Pearson in a project that I have been working on."

"What is the nature of the project?"

"It is to do with a Roman temple that used to stand on the outskirts of Weyford."

"Was Dr Pearson interested in your project?"

"She was. She suggested another person who may be better placed to take it forward."

"And what time did you conclude your meeting?"

"Shortly before five o'clock. I remember hearing the news headlines soon after I left."

"During your meeting with Dr Pearson, did either

of you refer to any documents or objects that may have been in her possession?"

"There was a file with some pictures copied from an old book. Pictures of the temple."

"Anything else?"

"Not that I remember."

"Did you bring anything into the room with you?"

"My laptop. And a folder of papers."

"Did you refer to these during your meeting?"

"I did."

"Do you recall seeing a lump of concrete anywhere in the room?"

"Yes, there was one on her desk."

"Did you touch it?"

"I moved it when I showed Dr Pearson a film on my laptop."

"We may want to check the files on your laptop. Please do not make any alterations to them, or delete anything. What was the nature of the material in the files?"

"They were to do with the proposal we were discussing."

"Did you see anyone else on your visit? Anyone either inside the building, or outside when you arrived or left?"

"I don't remember seeing anyone."

"When you arrived, how did you gain access to the building? Was the front door open, or locked?"

"It was locked. I had to press the intercom, and Dr Pearson admitted me."

"And when you left, was the door open or locked?"

"I believe it was locked. I turned the latch – it has a Yale type lock."

"And when the door closed, would you say that it locked itself after you?"

"I couldn't say for sure. It has a spring, so I would assume it did."

"Did Dr Pearson accompany you to the door?"

"No, she remained in her office, on the upper level."

"Was there any disagreement between you during the meeting?"

"No. She was polite and professional. We parted amicably."

The questioning continued in the same vein for several more minutes. A transcript of the interview was drawn up which Paul was asked to sign and then, "Thank you Mr Conrad, you are free to go now. Please remain where we can make contact with you. There may be some further issues that we will want to question you about. We may seek a warrant to view the files on your computer and your mobile phone."

Paul walked back to the car where Caroline was waiting for him. "You look absolutely shell-shocked," she said. She edged into the traffic, and they began their journey home. The mood was charged with concern.

"While you were at the police station I spoke to a journalist on the *Surrey Messenger*," she said. "He couldn't tell me a lot, but he said that Dr Pearson's body was discovered on Friday morning by a cleaner."

"What had happened to her? Do they know?"

"He couldn't say for sure, but she was found dead in her office. He thinks her head had been bashed in, with a large stone or something. The police aren't giving much away."

"They asked me about the piece of concrete I gave her – with the mosaic bits in."

There was a long silence.

"You don't suppose that was the murder weapon?" said Caroline.

"I don't know. They didn't say. Did you find out when the murder took place?"

"The journalist got the impression that she'd been dead for over twelve hours."

Another silence, then Caroline asked the question she had been dreading.

"They don't think you did it, do they?"

"I don't know. I think they're talking to all the people who saw her on Thursday. They'll probably want to question me again."

—⟨∞⟩—

A week later, the police were back. This time they called in person at the London home of Paul and Caroline. And this time there were no pleasantries.

"Mr Conrad, I am arresting you on suspicion of the murder of Dr Margaret Pearson. You do not have to say anything, but it may harm your defence if you do not mention when questioned something which you later rely on in court. Anything you do say may be given in evidence."

"But, that's ridiculous. I didn't kill her! I'm trying to stop it!"

Caroline watched helplessly as Paul was taken away. She went back into the house and gave way to tears of fear, frustration and anger.

"I must press you on this point, Mr Conrad. You said, when you were arrested, 'But that's ridiculous. I'm trying to stop it.' What are you trying to stop, Mr Conrad?" The detective sergeant was persistent in her questioning.

"I can't tell you."

"Mr Conrad, you are not helping your case by continuing to avoid answering my questions."

Paul sat silent, staring blankly at the bare wall of the interview room. It was cramped and claustrophobic.

Above, a single neon tube cast a harsh light. In the centre was a table on which stood a recording machine. Four chairs were set opposite each other in pairs. Paul and his solicitor sat facing the interviewing officer.

"Let me ask you about your laptop files. We have discovered that during the time when you say you were in a meeting with Dr Pearson, a video file was accessed which appears to show the demolition, using explosives, of a large house. What can you tell me about that?"

"It stood on the site where the Roman temple used to be."

"The temple that you were meeting Dr Pearson about? The project that you referred to?"

"Yes."

"You appear to have a large number of files relating to concrete on the laptop. Why is that?"

"It is a research interest of mine."

"We have learned from her colleagues that when you met Dr Pearson the first time, the subject of concrete was also raised. How did that come about?"

"We were visiting the site where the house used to stand. The house in the film. It was built of concrete."

"And that is also the site where the temple used to stand?"

"Yes."

"What did Dr Pearson tell you about the temple that day?"

"She found pieces of the temple in the concrete of the house."

"How did she react when she discovered that?"

"She was angry."

"She was more than angry, wasn't she, Mr Conrad? Did she not say that, in her opinion, it was one of the greatest acts of cultural vandalism of the nineteenth century?"

"She did say something like that, yes." God, they've been thorough, thought Paul.

"And she held one of your ancestors responsible."

"My great-grandfather, yes."

"How did you react to that?"

"At the time I remember finding it quite amusing."

"But you don't find it amusing now, do you, Mr Conrad?"

"Not after everything that's happened, no."

The detective leant towards Paul.

"And just what has happened?"

"I can't tell you that."

"Why not, Mr Conrad?"

"You wouldn't believe me."

Paul's solicitor turned to him. "You don't need to say anything that you don't want to," he said. The questioning continued.

"These things that have happened. Are they the things you said you were trying to stop?"

There was a long silence.

"Whatever it is, Mr Conrad, it would be much better to get it off your chest. What has happened? What are you trying to stop?"

Paul felt himself losing his grip. The questioning had been going on all day, and he could hardly stand any more. He heard a voice, his own, say in a low tone, "The murders."

"The murders? Who is committing these murders?"

Paul looked up, first at the detective, and then at the chair next to her, where a shadowy figure was manifesting. It was a face he knew well, and it smiled at him and nodded slowly.

"She is!" He pointed at the chair. "She is!"

The detective was visibly shaken and sought to calm the situation.

"And who is she?"

"Alecto of course! Look at her! Alecto!"

"I request that my client not answer any more questions," said his solicitor.

"Mr Conrad, I am going to halt the interview at this point. I suggest that you lie down for a while, and we will arrange for you to receive some medical help."

The detective called for a colleague, and Paul was taken back to the police cell. There were hurried conversations, and the detective reached for the telephone and made several urgent calls.

A Friend in Need

"My dear, do come in!" Julia Fielding took Caroline's coat and ushered her into the sitting room. "You poor things, what an awful thing to happen."

"I suppose you read about it in the *Messenger*," said Caroline.

"It's been all over the news – and Paul! I can't believe it."

"You know they charged him yesterday, don't you?"

"I heard it on the Six O'Clock. And now they're linking him to Rosemary Nugent's death too. I just can't believe it."

"I hope you don't mind my coming to see you. There's no-one else I can talk to."

"Of course not. If there's anything I can do. Why don't you tell me about it, if you can?"

Caroline had slept little since Paul's arrest and subsequent detention in a secure psychiatric unit where he was being held for assessment. The news that he had been charged with the murder of Margaret Pearson had come as a further bombshell. Caroline was still in shock and sat rocking slightly on the edge of the armchair.

"The worst thing is, there's so much circumstantial evidence," she said. "They did a DNA test on the lump of concrete, and of course they found Paul's all over it."

"That's the murder weapon, is it?"

"Apparently. But the DNA was only there because he picked it up and gave it to her at the site, and he also moved it during their meeting. He swears he didn't hit her with it."

"Was he the last person to see her alive?"

"The police think so. The time of death was put at around the time Paul was there. When the cleaner opened up, the door was locked; the security cameras show that no-one had entered the building after Paul left, and there was no sign of forcible entry. She'd been dead for over twelve hours when they found her." Caroline had begun to shiver, despite the blazing fire in the grate. Julia Fielding took a crocheted shawl and wrapped it round her guest's shoulders.

"And they're saying such horrible things. They say he did it because Dr Pearson insulted his great-grandfather. And that's so untrue. We laughed about that at the time. Paul's the last person who could do anything like that."

"And what about the Law lecturer? What are the police saying about her death?"

"That's awful – it just gets worse and worse. Apparently Paul got overwrought and started telling them about the things we told you – about Alexis Tobin, and all that. So they went and questioned her. She said she wasn't even at the Ferndown estate that day. You can imagine what their response was to being told that Alexis Tobin is really a Roman Fury. They're now suggesting that Paul is some sort of fantasising psychopath who assumes the identity of Alecto when he commits these murders. Oh Julia, I wish we'd never got mixed up in it. I wish we'd never gone near that place." Caroline was on the verge of tears but managed to stay controlled.

"Why did you and Paul set up the meeting with Dr Pearson?" asked Julia.

"We wanted to get her help. Paul had this idea that if we could rebuild the temple in virtual reality, using a computer program, we could appeal to Juno to stop all the horrors. And Dr Pearson knows – knew – some people who could do it. It sounds so silly now, doesn't it?" Caroline put her face in her hands and wept.

Julia sat close opposite her and took her hands. "Caroline, look at me. Do you think that Paul murdered Margaret Pearson?"

"No. No. When he came home from the meeting, he was his usual self. If he'd done what they're accusing him of, I would have known. He can't hide things very well. I would have known."

"I don't believe he did it either. From what I know of him, Paul isn't capable of that sort of thing."

"So who did do it? And how?"

"Why don't we, for the sake of argument, stay with your original theory? That the house, or the site, has got some sort of jinx on it. I'm not saying I believe it, but let's work it through. Several people, myself included, have had some sort of strange experience there, haven't they? And you yourself saw the film with Juno, and then with Alecto, didn't you?"

"Mmm." Caroline was happy to follow Julia's narrative. She had made the same mental journey herself, over and over, in the small hours of the morning.

"And we think that Alecto, or whatever it is, either killed off or drove mad some of the house's first inhabitants."

Caroline nodded assent.

"So if we assume she's still active, who might she want to have a go at next, after Rosemary Nugent?"

"Paul."

"Yes. Paul," said Julia. "The descendant of the man who destroyed the mosaic. You said that Alexis as good as told you that she knew who you were."

"She did. And she knows we can't tell anyone about it: they just wouldn't believe us," said Caroline picking up on Julia's train of thought. "She kills off Margaret Pearson in a way that makes Paul the obvious suspect and is calculated to cause him the absolute maximum distress. She's framed him for murder, and now she's trying to drive him mad, like she did Henry Maddox. Nightmares, torment and despair. It's got her fingerprints all over it."

"And nobody will believe it, will they?" said Julia.

"That's just the point. Because Paul's defence – that there's a Roman Fury on the loose – is also the case for the prosecution: that he's a looney-tunes psychopath. It's the perfect crime, committed by the perfect criminal. An Ancient Fury. You've got to hand it to her, haven't you?" For the first time that afternoon, some of Caroline's old spirit showed through.

"And another thing: by killing Margaret Pearson she's neatly kyboshed our idea of creating the temple in virtual reality. The company that could do it was set up by a group of Margaret Pearson's ex-students. Why would they go out of their way to help the person accused of her murder?"

"Remember though, what Henry Maddox wrote in the book. 'Only she can make it stop.' I still think that an appeal to Juno is the best route to helping Paul," said Julia Fielding. She sat back in her chair. Caroline thought for a while before replying.

"I think I'll have to get back in touch with Sandra Thorne. She's the person who can do the virtual reality. Somehow I have to convince her of this."

"It may not be easy. If you need me to corroborate anything, just say the word."

"Thank you. I can't tell you how much it's meant just to be able to talk about it with someone who doesn't think I'm looney-tunes too."

"When are you seeing Paul next?"

"At the weekend."

"Give him my love. Tell him I believe in him."

"I will." Caroline rose to put on her coat.

"Julia, I hope we can see this through."

Fenestra Virtuality

The days passed for Caroline in a haze of disbelief and unhappiness, and there was no remission from the living nightmare that now engulfed her and Paul. After the psychiatric report, Paul's subsequent appearance at the committal proceedings, and his detention on remand in a secure hospital – for his own good, they were told – there seemed little hope of a reversal of their fortunes. Caroline's nights were filled with endless rehearsals of different explanations of their predicament, and her visits to Paul gave her little comfort from the dreaded and, it seemed, inevitable outcome. What jury could possibly believe the confection that constituted his defence when faced with the grim reality of the evidence?

"Be brave," they said to each other, but when apart again they felt afraid.

The bond between Caroline and Julia Fielding became stronger. "Sometimes I think without you I couldn't face it," she said on one of their regular telephone conversations. Julia could do little about the nightmares and torment that afflicted Caroline, but she did much to save her from the last of Alecto's visitations, despair.

Caroline's intention to involve Sandra Thorne at Fenestra Virtuality was strong, but at first she held back from making contact for fear of a refusal. A second rejection from Sandra would be final and with it would go her last hope for saving Paul. Yet she knew that at some time she would have to make that call, and she spent hours imagining how the conversation might go.

The issue was resolved unexpectedly one morning by the telephone ringing. These days she screened all her incoming calls to escape the persistence of the press, and when she heard the name of the caller, her heart missed a beat. "This is Sandra Thorne at Fenestra Virtuality. Could you please give me a ring . . ."

"Sandra, this is Caroline," she said, picking up the phone. It was the first time they had spoken since meeting at the Ferndown site, when Sandra had identified the mosaic pieces in the concrete. Their reintroduction over, Sandra came to the point.

"We are working on re-imagining the Weyford temple. It's our way of honouring Margaret Pearson. A sort of digital festschrift, if you like. Many of us here were taught by her, so it seemed the right thing to do."

"Why are you calling me?" asked Caroline.

Sandra did not answer her question directly. "When Paul emailed us about the temple, he had a reason why we should work on it, which he said he would tell us in person. Can you tell me what that reason was?"

Caroline hesitated. "I don't think I could on the telephone. It's rather complicated."

"Would you be prepared to visit us?"

"Of course."

A date was set. Caroline put the phone down and immediately picked it up again.

"Julia, it's Caroline. I've just had a call from Sandra Thorne at Fenestra. They want me to visit them. They're working on the temple. It's what we asked them to do – but they're doing it for a different reason. I can't wait to tell Paul!"

Caroline's train to Cambridge eased its way out of King's Cross. For the next hour she went over the pitch that she would make to Sandra, the case for her involvement in whatever they were doing. Her new fear was that she might be denied access to the finished result of Fenestra's work on the temple, denied the opportunity to make an appeal to its titular goddess: so near, and yet so far. A taxi took her to the northern outskirts of the city where a series of silver-coloured buildings were strung along the ring road. Fenestra Virtuality was in a small office block sandwiched between two hangar-like sheds, surrounded by grass and newly-planted shrubs.

The interior did not conform to Caroline's expectations. She had imagined a bustling studio environment with large computer screens offering rich visual imagery portraying the company's product. What she saw was several rows of desks in a large open-plan space, their occupants seemingly engaged in entering data into banks of computers. It could be a utility company's call centre, she thought. The only thing that suggested a more creative dimension to the business was a video camera mounted in front of a green-screen drape at the far end of the room, with a rack of studio lights above.

Sandra Thorne ushered Caroline into a glass-walled meeting room. She anticipated Caroline's reaction. "Not quite what you expected?" she said. "A lot of people say that. What we do is at the cutting edge of virtual reality, but in the background there is a massive database – a huge silo of machine-code. That's what they're working on," she said, gesturing to the room beyond. "Of course, the user doesn't see all that."

She poured Caroline a cup of coffee, and they sat down at the conference table. "I'm going to bring Michael Dunbar in. He's the other guy you met with Margaret on the temple site." She picked up a telephone. "Michael, Caroline's here, if you'd like to join us. Thanks."

Michael Dunbar was a tall, angular man in his early thirties with heavy black-framed glasses. He was dressed in a black polo-neck shirt and black trousers. Caroline recognised him immediately from their earlier encounter. So now two of the three people she had met previously were present. It could be awkward, thought Caroline, to avoid mentioning what had happened to Margaret and Paul's alleged involvement.

Sandra spoke first. "Before we say why we've asked you to visit us, I'd like to tell you a bit about what we do." She settled into a script she had delivered many times. "We set up Fenestra for two purposes. The first is what we call the gamification of the cultural heritage."

Caroline looked blank.

"That's just jargon for finding new ways of making the past come alive," Sandra continued. "When you visit a historic site, there's usually a guide book to read as you go round, or an audio commentary, or a board showing how it might have looked. None of which is particularly exciting for the visitor. We model the site in 3D and superimpose on it a realisation of how it would have looked at a previous time. Our reconstruction is offered to the visitor, who wears a special headset to view it. That can be either on site or at a distance, so you could 'visit' a historic place without leaving your living room and walk around it using our technology. It's called augmented reality. To make it more fun, we add avatars, characters from the past, into the buildings. You can talk to them, and they tell you about their lives and about the buildings."

"So it's like a historical computer game, then?" said Caroline.

"Something like that, yes, but we do try to get it as historically accurate as possible."

"What's the second purpose?"

"We predict that virtual tourism will really take off in the next few years. We intend to use the revenue from it to create a library of historic buildings that are at risk – from wars, or terrorism or geographical change – earthquakes, or rivers being dammed, for example. We have close links with the University, and we work with them to create virtual copies of these sites. So on the one hand, we have the popular tourist destinations re-imagined for a new generation, and on the other we have world-class monuments that are under threat preserved for academic study in a virtual environment."

"And where does the Weyford temple fit into all this?" Caroline asked, anxious to get to the point of her visit. Michael picked up her question.

"We're commissioning the next generation of software which will soon be the platform for all our projects. It's so far ahead of anything that anyone else has that we believe it will become the industry standard. We were looking for a building that we could use to test it on when we heard of Margaret's – of Margaret's murder."

Caroline sensed his unease. "Paul didn't do it, you know. He'd never do a thing like that," she said.

"Could we put that aside for the moment?" said Sandra. "After all, you presumably contacted me before you knew it had happened."

"That's true."

Michael continued, "Margaret was head of the archaeology department when we were at University, and we all owe a lot to her. When she retired to Weyford, she became interested in the Temple of Juno – and that's how we got involved in the site exploration. It was her pet project. It also happens to be ideal for the testing we need to do, so we decided we would pay tribute to her by creating a virtual version of it. We have a good description of it; some excellent plates of the mosaic floor; and a lot of additional material that she had researched, so it was a relatively straightforward piece of work. We've been working at it non-stop for the last three weeks."

"So why did you invite me here today, if it's all so straightforward?" asked Caroline.

Sandra replied, "We will answer that, but could we do it the other way round – and you tell us first why you emailed us? Why you wanted us to build the temple in virtual reality?"

For the next half hour Caroline recounted the story of their research and the succession of unexplained events that had led them to conclude that the destruction of the temple remains was linked to several deaths, some back in past centuries, and now, horribly, in this.

"And we believe that somehow Juno's curse is behind it all, and if we could only make a direct appeal to her to call off her attack dog Alecto, we might be able to sort it all out. That's how Paul came up with the idea of rebuilding the temple. And now Paul's been charged with murder, it's our last chance."

Sandra and Michael listened without interrupting, taking in every word.

"Thank you, Caroline. I'll now tell you why we wanted to talk to you," said Sandra. "Another coffee?" She refilled the cups and continued.

"I mentioned that we build avatars into our virtual environments. They look very natural – they're actually based on real people. We do motion-capture imaging of actors to make them even more realistic. And they can converse. We use some of the latest artificial intelligence software, so they don't just parrot scripted sentences. It's sometimes hard to believe that they're not real people. It's like having your own personal tour guide – from the period of the building you're visiting.

"We created an avatar for the Roman temple. Calybe, the priestess, she's called. We gave her a database of knowledge and a vocabulary. And we hired an elderly character actress to do her moves. She is very convincing. She's one of our best creations, I'd say."

"I'd love to see her," said Caroline.

"But we have a problem with her," continued Sandra. "When we started the beta testing stage – that's running the program before we sign it off – we noticed that she had a habit of going off-message. Some of the things she said were quite creepy. And she was using words that weren't in the vocabulary we gave her. Theoretically there's no way that can happen in our software."

"You mean, she was acquiring a life of her own?"

"It was a bit like that, yes. It had our programmers completely baffled. And then something else happened that really did spook us. Michael, do you want to tell Caroline about it?"

"I'll try. I was doing some work on the temple project one evening. I called up Calybe and started talking to her. She always wears a robe with a hood. We never filmed the actress without the hood up. While I was talking to her, Calybe pushed her hood off. Underneath, her head was covered in snakes." Michael's voice hinted at the shock he still felt from the experience.

Caroline reached into the portfolio she had brought with her and pulled out the screengrab that Paul had made from the film. "Did she look like this?"

Michael looked at the image. "Yes, that's her all right. Her face is more wizened, but I'd recognise those snakes anywhere. It was pretty frightening, I can tell you. Where does this image come from?"

"From the last frames of the film I told you about. The first time we looked at it there was an image of Juno superimposed on it, and the second time, her – Alecto."

"And as we know, she's also in the mosaic floor," said Sandra.

"I still don't understand why you asked me to come here, though," said Caroline. Sandra came to the point.

"You probably know that the police came to question us about what happened when we met you on the temple site, and of course we followed the story of Paul's being arrested and charged."

"You don't believe he did it, do you?"

"No," said Sandra. "We know he didn't. That's why we had to get in touch with you. You see, Alecto has confessed to it."

TESTING TIMES

The visiting centre was a large high-ceilinged room with tall windows that looked out over parkland. Twelve square tables with seats fixed to the floor accommodated patients and their visitors, and at popular times the room was crowded and noisy. Caroline checked in at reception and made her way across to where Paul was sitting. The hour they had together on these occasions was precious, but left both feeling drained and disoriented.

"How did your meeting with Graham go?" asked Caroline. Paul's solicitor had visited the previous day to go over his defence.

"About as well as you could expect. He's now talking about a plea of diminished responsibility. That way I could be tried for manslaughter rather than murder. I told him what he could do with it. I didn't kill her. You know that, don't you?"

"Of course I do. I believe you. And so do lots of other people."

"How did you get on at Fenestra?"

"I hardly know where to start. They've built the temple, Paul. And they're on our side."

Caroline recounted her visit to the Cambridge company, ending with Michael Dunbar's frightening experience. "It's another masterstroke by Alecto. The building that Fenestra have created in honour of Margaret Pearson is haunted by her murderer," she concluded. "Michael said she didn't just confess to the murder, she positively gloated over it."

"Because she knows that she can never be brought to book for it. You can't put an avatar in the dock, can you?" said Paul.

"No, but we are much further forward," said Caroline. "For one thing, we have two more people who are now convinced that the whole thing is real and not in your imagination. And they want to do something about it – if only to get their temple out of the clutches of Alecto."

Paul laughed. It was the first time Caroline had seen him lighten up since his arrest. "How are they proposing to do that?"

"I don't know yet. But Sandra did say she'd get back to me."

"It won't help me much though, will it?"

"Paul, this was your idea, and now it's happening. Remember, 'Only she can make it stop'."

"Can she? Do you really think so?"

"I honestly don't know. But I still think it's our best hope."

—◦◦◦—

The following week found Caroline retracing her steps to Cambridge.

"What we're proposing is quite high risk," said Sandra Thorne. "We simply don't know what will happen."

"Margaret Pearson told Paul that she didn't believe in the power of ancient curses," said Caroline.

"I wonder if she'd say the same thing now. Personally, I'm going to keep an open mind. Michael, can you talk Caroline through the plan?"

"We'd normally do this only after a lot more testing, but we propose to do a full on-site appraisal of the virtual temple. That means aligning it with the co-ordinates of the original building, which fortunately we know very accurately. It will then remain anchored to that point, and we will be able to view it at full resolution and move around it and within it. Effectively it will appear to us as if it's really there. For safety's sake I have de-activated the Calybe avatar."

"And what about Juno?"

"She's just a statue. We haven't created any virtual identity for her."

"How do we view the temple?" asked Caroline.

"All you need are these," said Sandra, handing Caroline a slip case. Inside was a pair of what looked like ordinary spectacles. "They're the latest generation. No more bulky headsets. The lenses have a thin coating that creates the images, and the earpieces are at the ends of the arms. All the electronics are in the frame."

"And once we're inside, I can make some sort of offering to Juno, like the Romans did?"

"If that's what you feel is right, yes."

"I'd like to bring a friend of mine. She's the person I told you about who saw the little girl in the villa," said Caroline. "It's too bad Paul can't be with us."

"He can be, if you can give him those glasses," said Michael. "Not physically, of course, unless they let him out. But as long as there's a mobile signal wherever he is, he'll be able to see what we're seeing and hear what we're hearing. He just won't be able to join in – we're still developing that functionality."

Caroline left with the glasses, and a range of dates.

In the following week she made two more visits. The first was to drop off the spectacles at the hospital, where they were accepted without question as Paul's reading glasses.

"I wish I could be there," said Paul, after Caroline had outlined the plan.

"So do I. Try not to worry too much, it is only a computer. And they've switched off Calybe, for safety."

"Well, good luck. And I'll see you afterwards."

"Mmm. Bye now." Caroline rose to leave. She hoped that she had not revealed her anxiety; after all, Paul could do nothing except watch. And, maybe, pray.

Her other visit was to Julia Fielding.

Julia was dressed in outdoor clothes. "Why don't we go for a walk?" she said. "Maisie needs some exercise, and it's a lovely day." They drove to a local beauty spot.

"So what am I supposed to do, once we're in the temple? I've never made a supplication to a Roman goddess before," Caroline said, as they negotiated a stile leading onto open downland.

"No, it's not really an everyday experience, is it?"

"I don't even know which Juno we're dealing with. Margaret Pearson told Paul that there are lots of different sides to her, and that seems to be something of an understatement." She took a piece of paper from her pocket. "There's Juno Caprotina, Juno Sospita, Juno Curitis, Juno Moneta, Juno Lucina, it goes on and on."

"Does it matter?" asked Julia.

"Well, one of them's armed and dangerous; one's all about fertility; and another one protects people – especially women. I think I'd settle for her, right now."

"And you don't know which of them this temple was dedicated to?"

"No. Margaret Pearson told Paul that she thought the missing corner of the mosaic held the clue, so we'll probably never find out."

"You're taking this augmented reality thing very seriously, aren't you?" said Julia.

"I have to, Julia. I mean, if you look at it objectively, it's absolutely daft to think that I can get Paul off a murder charge by appealing to an ancient deity. But when you put it in the context of what's happened, it maybe makes some sense. I'm just not sure how to go about it; and I've got to get it right."

"I have a feeling that you'll know what to do when the time comes."

"I hope so, Julia. I do hope so."

A Date with the Deities

From the window of the master bedroom of the Ferndown Estate show house Alexis Tobin surveyed the view. The skies were clear, and the sun on the Surrey landscape caught the tops of the hills in the morning light. She sensed the approach of the day's protagonists: two from Cambridge who would set the stage, and two others who would play their parts upon it, who presumed to thwart her in her demonic assignment. She reached for her phone and tweeted, "A good day to do Her bidding. Special event at Ferndown Estate.   One more will complete on a new home today. #NTD."   It was time for some more havoc.

She watched, hidden from view, as Michael Dunbar parked in one of the visitor bays, then walked with Sandra Thorne to the turning circle at the end of a short cul-de-sac. It had been coned off ready for their arrival.

"You can hardly recognise it from the last time, can you?" he said. "But the GPS can't be wrong. This is definitely where it stood."

The next half hour was taken up with entering data into a laptop, walking, measuring, checking, until the two were satisfied that all the co-ordinates were correctly logged. Michael took off his heavy black-framed glasses and put on the lightweight pair.

"That's pretty good," he said. Sandra put on hers.

"Wow," she said.

Deep in the earth, and across the centuries, ancient spirits were awakened, and old memories stirred.

Caroline and Julia turned from the Weyford one-way system onto the Portsmouth Road and began the climb out of town towards the Ferndown estate.

"We've got a nice day for it. How long do you think we'll be there?" asked Julia.

"I've no idea, but I imagine the Cambridge team will want to get back at a reasonable time, and you know what the motorway can be like."

They drove past the bus stop where Rosemary Nugent had been found dead of a snakebite and turned up into the lanes that led to the estate. Caroline felt a pang of apprehension. Would Alexis Tobin still be there? Surely all the houses would have been sold by now, and she would have moved on.

"Did you bring any offerings?" asked Julia.

"I did. I went on a website about Roman gods, and there was a page on what to offer them if you don't want to sacrifice chickens. It said wine and cakes were good."

"And that's what you've brought?"

"Well, I thought we could always have them

afterwards. So I went to the off-licence and got a couple of bottles of Chianti, and then I baked some brownies."

The two women laughed. "It's the thought that counts, I suppose," said Julia.

At the appointed time they parked next to the Fenestra car, and Caroline introduced Julia. Michael handed them the special glasses.

"When you put these on, it will take a minute or two for them to capture the signal. Then you'll see the temple in front of you. It doesn't go further than the edge of the road, so you can walk around safely. I'd suggest you don't take them on and off as it can be disorientating if the temple keeps appearing and disappearing. When you go inside, you'll notice that the acoustic changes. The software knows the shape of the interior and what it's made of, and it creates an acoustic to match."

"That's clever," said Caroline.

"OK, is everyone ready?" said Sandra. "Let's go."

And at the same time, in his room at the hospital, Paul put on his pair of spectacles.

At first there was nothing to see, as Michael had predicted. Then the view of the houses in the cul-de-sac changed, as in the foreground a new building appeared.

"Oh my goodness," said Julia.

"It's just amazing," said Caroline.

And sixty miles away her husband said, very quietly, "It works, it works."

The temple was some thirty feet tall with eighteen Corinthian columns arranged in a circle, forming its periphery. The columns stood on a low plinth and above them a circular cornice supported a shallow pantile roof with, in the centre, a dome finished with a finial in the shape of a pinecone. To the viewers it appeared solid, and every bit as real as the houses of the new estate with which it shared its site.

Caroline walked towards the temple. It remained anchored to the ground as she moved round it. She turned back to look at the new houses and saw to her surprise a small group of people walking determinedly towards the temple. All were in antique dress, some in long flowing gowns, others in short knee-length tunics. They were led by a young man dressed in a tunic cinched in at the waist by a leather belt, carrying a drinking horn. They approached the four visitors and stopped, staring. The curiosity was mutual.

"Michael, are these people your creation?" asked Sandra. He turned and looked at the new arrivals. "Absolutely not," he said. He addressed the leader, "Hi, I'm Michael."

"Is this anything to do with you?" came the reply. "The temple."

"You mean you can see it?" said Michael. "How?"

"We've got eyes, haven't we?" said the man. "And it wasn't there yesterday. Did you put it there?"

"Sort of," said Michael. "It's a copy of the temple to Juno that was here in ancient times."

"Course it is, you don't need to tell me that. It's not bad." He looked the temple up and down. "Needs a bit more bronze on it, and the roof's the wrong colour, but you've done a decent enough job. Is She in there?"

"She?"

"Juno. It's her temple after all, isn't it?"

Julia could contain her curiosity no longer. "Would you mind telling us who you all are?"

"I'm the Head Lar. And this is Vesta. She looks after the hearths. And these are the Penates. They do the pantries."

Sandra's eyes widened in astonishment. "You're the Lares and Penates? The household gods?"

"That's us. I'm surprised you've even heard of us. No-one else pays us any attention round here. It was bad enough when we had just the one villa to look after, but now we've got this lot," and he gestured to the new estate, "We're just not staffed for that. And they pay no attention to us. I haven't had a libation in, I don't know how long." He made a move towards the temple. "Now, if you don't mind, we need to get in there. She's the only one that can sort it all out."

Caroline tensed with anxiety. Once the household gods were in the temple, there was no knowing how long they would be. She might never get a look-in. "Wait a minute," she said.   The household gods stopped and looked at her.

"Did you say you hadn't had any offerings recently?"

"I'll say," said the Head Lar. "We took up residence here, what, nearly a century-and-a-half ago. It's been a long time."

"I've brought you something." Caroline put down her hold-all in front of the gods and pulled out the bottles of Chianti and a plastic box containing the brownies. "Here, try one." She offered them round. The Head Lar picked up a bottle and, after a little experimentation, unscrewed the cap and poured the wine into his drinking horn.

"Now that's more like it," he said. "I can tell you're a lady of great understanding." He took a long swig from the horn. "Very nice. Very nice indeed."

Vesta bit into one of Caroline's brownies. "We have been dishonoured and neglected for too long," she said. "Your offerings are most welcome in this unholy place."

As the Penates passed the brownies round, Caroline took Michael and Sandra to one side. "Keep them talking, can you? Otherwise we'll never get into the temple."

"You bet we will. They could be the best avatars we've ever had." Michael took a small video camera from his bag and approached the household gods. "Can we have a quick chat before you go in to the temple?" he said.

"Quick!" said Caroline to Julia. "We may not have much time."

The two women moved silently towards the temple. The illusion of mass and substance was sustained as they entered it. Caroline put out a hand to touch the massive door, bound in bronze, which stood open at the threshold. She was surprised that her touch was not met with resistance but instead passed straight through it. Once they were inside, the door closed with a loud clanging thud which echoed around the interior. Michael had been right about the acoustic: it made the virtual building seem almost real.

When their eyes had adjusted to the lower light levels, they could see that they were standing in the inner sanctum of the temple. On the far side, opposite the door, stood a statue on a plinth, about twice life-size. Above them was a domed ceiling, painted dark blue and illuminated with stars and planets. On the walls either side of the statue were a series of bronze panels depicting scenes of women bearing gifts. The temple was lit by flaming torches fixed to the wall, which cast flickering shadows on the bas-reliefs. Between the panels, opposite each other, were two altars. The entire floor was taken up with the mosaic depicting Juno, resplendent in a flowing blue gown with a diadem in her hair, the peacock glowing in green and blue at her side. Caroline hardly dared to look at the face of the Fury to the right of the goddess's head. The other side showed a blank area where once another image had complemented the whole. Whoever had created the virtual floor had stopped short of interpolating a replacement for the missing area.

"It's incredible, Caroline. And to think it's all an optical illusion." Julia's voice was hushed.

Caroline was standing below the plinth, looking up at the giant figure of the goddess. "Look, she doesn't have a spear," she said. "She's holding a dish. And some sort of sceptre in her right hand."

"What does that mean?" asked Julia.

"I think it means that the temple is dedicated to her as a protector, rather than a warrior, but I can't be sure."

"So what do we do now?"

Julia's question was answered by a sound from behind them. They turned and saw coming through the door a well-dressed young woman with long dark hair. Again the door closed with a sound that reverberated in the chamber. The newcomer spoke.

"Mrs Conrad, what a pleasure. I did so hope you would return."

Caroline recognised her instantly. Of course. Alexis Tobin. Why had she thought she would not be here? She rounded on her.

"I know who you are. You can drop that phoney disguise now, you old hag."

Julia looked startled at Caroline's language. "She's Alexis – Alecto," Caroline said to her under her breath.

"Is she real?"

"Very. I think."

"An old hag am I? Then let's see what havoc hags can wreak!"

The svelte young figure of Alexis began to transform into the monstrous shape of the Fury. Now she appeared in her most hideous form, her eyes rolling, her hair a mass of hissing snakes, but still alert and agile. She pulled a torch from its fixture on the wall and waved it in the two women's faces.

"I bring you death from the Furies' pit. This is how your life will end, and then I shall receive my dues from Her." She waved the torch in the direction of the statue. "She set me on, and I will do Her work."

Caroline had finally had enough. Ignoring the flaming torch and the hissing serpents, she strode to the centre of the mosaic floor, and with arms akimbo she addressed the Fury.

"Since I have no way of knowing what is real here, and what is not, I will say just this. Whatever happened here was long ago and should not still be blighting lives today. Whoever lived here did not deserve to die. You, Alecto, are nothing more than a walking virus, and we would all be well shot of you. It's time to wrap it up. Time to move on." She turned her back on the Fury and paced across the floor, stopping in front of the statue of Juno. Her anger emboldened her to address the giant figure that towered over her. Looking directly up into the face of the statue she cast aside all caution and continued her tirade.

"And how could you allow innocent people to die? How could you stand by while good people are tormented by her?" (And here she swept her arm towards Alecto). "OK, it was a beautiful floor, and it's a shame what happened to it, but you have set this creature to deal out death and despair wherever she goes. She has driven people mad. An innocent woman has died horribly from her venom. My husband is facing a murder trial because she framed him. I beseech you now to put a stop to it before anyone else gets hurt!"

In his room at the psychiatric hospital Paul sat watching the events of the day play out on his augmented reality glasses. He saw around the temple, heard the Head Lar's complaints, and followed Caroline and Julia into the inner sanctum. He could do nothing to influence the action; he was a mere spectator. Even so, he could not help but comment out loud.

"Take care, Caroline, you know who she is," he said when Alexis entered. And he cringed when Alecto assumed her true shape. He did not hear the door of his room being opened, and the nurse entering.

"Oh no, don't say that!" said Paul.

"Who is saying something, Mr Conrad?"

Paul looked up, his face drawn with dread. "My wife has just berated Juno."

"Who is Juno?"

"She's the Queen of the gods, of course. And now Alecto will kill her with a snake."

"Alecto will kill Juno?"

"No, she'll kill my wife."

The nurse closed the door quietly and spoke to a doctor.

"Poor Mr Conrad is unwell. It's the snakes again, I'm afraid."

—⁊⊶⊱—

Before the echo of her outburst had died away, Caroline was overcome with anguish and remorse. What had possessed her to harangue the goddess instead of appealing to her compassion as she had intended? And she had given the offerings intended for Juno to the Lares and Penates. What possible mercy could she expect, what remission from the suffering, what reversal of fortune, now that she had thrown away their only hope of salvation? How could it all have gone so horribly wrong? In this her darkest moment she gave way for the first time to Alecto's cruellest affliction, despair. 'If there's one goddess you wouldn't want to get on the wrong side of, it's Juno': the words she had used at Julia Fielding's rang in her ears. How could the goddess overlook her outburst? What punishment might she inflict for such *lèse-majesté*? Surely nothing now could save Paul, or her, from their fate.

Alecto gloried in Caroline's agony: now that she had separated her from her husband, she could work on both of them more easily. Caroline's diatribe against Juno was more than the Fury could have hoped for: by insulting the goddess, she had fallen straight into her trap. Surely Juno would reward her for her demonic diligence.

"A walking virus, am I?" she shrieked at Caroline. "Then you shall feel what venom is in the virus; I shall brandish it, and you will feel its pain."

She plucked a snake from her scalp and, holding its tail in her right hand, whirled it round her head, fixing Caroline with her staring, bloodshot eyes.

Julia was the first to see what happened next. From behind the plinth of the statue slipped a figure that she remembered well, though she had not seen nor heard her in half a century: a young girl, wearing a dark green pleated dress. The girl darted towards Caroline and Julia and stood in front of them, facing Alecto defiantly.

"It's Lucy, the little girl I saw that day in the villa," Julia whispered to Caroline, and she put her arms round the girl's shoulders. Lucy looked up at her and then turned back to address the Fury, her clear voice ringing in the echoing acoustic of the temple.

"You shall not harm her, or if you do, you harm me too, and you will answer to Juno, my guardian."

Alecto paused, then, fired with rage, she whirled the snake faster and faster. "So be it!" she cried, and released her deadly weapon. The snake whistled through the air across the temple, its jaws open, its eyes focused on Caroline, who raised her arm to fend it off.

Just as the snake was about to reach its target, a loud voice, commanding and intense, rang out.

"Stop!"

The snake froze, stationary in the air, inches from Caroline's face. She could see down its throat, see its forked tongue stretching forward, see its fangs poised to inject their venom. And she watched as the snake changed, dematerialised, and fell in golden flakes at her feet.

All turned to look at the source of the command. The statue turned slowly towards them, the sculpted robes now fluid over supple limbs. The goddess's voice resounded from the high domed roof.

"I have heard your plea. It is enough.
The terror now must end. Alecto,
you whom I set to punish these wrongdoings,
have exceeded my command, and now must cease
your treachery. To you who have felt her lash

and fear a bitter destiny, I bring respite.
My anger has abated, and in this sacred place,
my temple now re-born, I make amends.
The fleeting hour I shall at Jove's behest renew,
and Lethe's spring shall wipe the slate of memory.
I charge you now, Daughter of the Night, begone!
Regain your hellish lair and trouble earth no more."

Alecto hissed resentment, plucked a handful of snakes from her hair and, grasping them in her right hand, shook her fist one last time at her human prey. As they watched, the hideous image in the mosaic fragmented, and the solid floor became insubstantial. From the void that opened up came a hollow rumbling roar, like vast river rapids deep in a narrow gorge. Alecto peered into the abyss in front of her, took one pace forward, and descended to the underworld. As the last vestige of her disappeared, the floor slowly re-formed into the grotesque serpent-haired face of the Fury.

Caroline and Julia felt a sense of relief, but in Caroline's mind it was tempered with anxiety: how could Juno's promise of respite help Paul in his extremity? She turned back to the plinth and saw, to her amazement, that it was empty. The giant form of the goddess had vanished. Both women stared in disbelief at the vacant pedestal. With a quick movement, Lucy detached herself from Julia's clasp and ran across the mosaic floor. She threw herself into the arms of a figure that stood in a pool of sunlight

streaming from a high window. Tall, majestic and
dignified, the Lady in Blue clasped the child to her like a
mother embracing her long-lost daughter. And above
them, carved in the stone over an altar, Caroline read a
Latin inscription that answered the question that had
troubled her for so long: IVNO LVCINA. Juno Lucina.

Julia tugged at Caroline's sleeve and indicated that
they should withdraw. They found a small room to the
rear of the temple. Caroline's mind was racing. Suddenly
everything had changed, and the explanation lay in those
two words. Juno Lucina, the bringer of light, the goddess
of childbirth, the protector of mothers, the vital force, the
fountain of energy. She it was to whom the temple was
dedicated. And now Caroline too felt the pain of her loss,
of the assault on the mosaic floor. Not the crushing into
concrete – that came later. No, there was a much earlier
loss: the ploughing-up of the lost corner, the image that
had complemented the Fury on the opposite side. Now
at last she knew what that image was. But this was not
the time to explain. For now, the two women were
content to hold each other, to share the grief and joy that
could befall even the Queen of the gods. They stood silent
for a while. Then, "It's time to go," said Caroline.

"Yes."

They went back into the temple's inner sanctum. At
first sight it appeared just as they had found it when they
first entered. The plinth was home once more to the giant

statue, which again had every appearance of solid stone. The sun had moved round and was now casting its light on the floor, on the great mosaic of the goddess. Caroline walked across it and called Julia over. "Look."

The blank area, the corner of the mosaic that had been left unfilled, was now complete. Framed by a garland of flowers, and lit by the rays of the afternoon sun, shone the face of a young girl. Her hair was fair, her eyes as blue as the feathers of the peacock. It was unmistakeably the face of Lucy. The mosaic was whole once more.

"Do you have any idea what has just happened?" asked Julia.

"I think so. I'll tell you on the way home," said Caroline. "We should leave now."

"Yes," said Julia, "Mustn't keep the Head Lar waiting."

As they stepped outside, Caroline felt heavy drops of water falling on her head. Such was the completeness of the illusion of the temple that she assumed she had stepped outside into a shower of rain. She looked up at the sky. It was cloudless. Puzzled, she looked around her.

She and Paul were standing at the foot of a steep rise in the land, which had been clear-felled of its tree cover. Tree trunks were stacked high in several places around the site, and the vegetation had been hacked back. Immediately in front of them, high above their heads at the top of the short escarpment, was the exposed length of a long retaining wall.

"I can't believe it," said Caroline. "It's exactly as it is in the drawing." She held up the print copied from *The Building News* and compared the two. "There are the steps, and one, two, three, four pillars either side." The wall was swept round at the corners and continued for some distance, containing and defining the original site of the villa. Halfway along the wall was a projection with steps either side leading up to a terrace. They walked up the steps to where the villa had once stood. In front of them the ground had been stripped of its green cover. Small fragments of concrete were visible in the earth. "The original terrace wall, still in place, after a hundred and fifty years. Amazing."

"I bet they're going to build houses here," said Paul. At the far end of the site a driveway leading to the main road had been sealed off by a section of metal mesh fencing to which a notice was attached. He walked over and read it.

"It's a planning notice – 'Proposed erection of twelve dwellings' – plus landscaping."

"So we've just got here in time," said Caroline. "I can't imagine they'll hang about now they've started clearing the site." They spent the next half hour photographing the acre or so of land from every possible angle, ending up back at the steps. Caroline focused her camera on the wall, and Paul pulled away some ivy. "You can see the way the concrete was cast," he said. "And it's covered with stucco, and lined to make it look like stone."

"That's what the traditionalists hated about this concrete, isn't it – making it look like something else," said Caroline. "Still, it's lasted quite well." She pulled more at the ivy that Paul had dislodged and took a close-up of the bare concrete with its squared-off lines cut into the surface.

"I suppose we ought to be getting home," said Paul. Caroline looked down at her feet, her eye caught by something glinting in the newly scraped earth. She dug at it with a small stick, easing it out of the soil.

"Look," she said, "It's a gold necklace." It gleamed dully in the early afternoon light. "It's pretty." She opened her water bottle to wash off the soil. "Oh! The clasp is a snake's head, and it's biting its tail. Isn't that clever!"

"Someone must have dropped it I suppose. Maybe they lived in the concrete villa," said Paul.

"Yes, it looks quite old." She put the necklace in her bag. "Do you think we should take it to a museum?"

"Probably. It might be even older."

They walked down the path towards their car.

They were approached by a group of five people, deep in conversation, led by a woman in a waxed jacket.

"Good afternoon," said Paul.

"Afternoon," said the leader, and as they walked on up the path she resumed her briefing. "Sandra and Peter, I'll ask you to mark out the grid, and then Michael, could you and Stephen make a start on the geophysics?"

"Of course, Margaret," came the reply.

The two groups continued in their opposite directions, one arriving, the other leaving.

"Do you think we need to come back tomorrow?" Caroline asked Paul, as they drove off.

"No. We've been lucky with the light," said Paul. "I can't see that we'd get anything better on another day, can you?"

–❧ *Finis* ❧–

Author's Note

Keen students of the history of concrete will recognise that this fictional story is based on a real building, and much else besides is also true. In 1870 the concrete pioneer Charles Drake built for the brewer John Madocks an Italianate villa called Fernlands on the outskirts of Chertsey. During its construction the remains of a Roman building and many Roman artefacts were discovered. The Madocks family lived at Fernlands only briefly, and, after several more occupants, the house was abandoned in 1919 and stood empty for many years. At the outbreak of the Second World War its tower was considered to be too conspicuous a landmark, and when all attempts to demolish it by conventional means failed, the army was called in to take it down with explosives. The rest of the house was demolished in the 1960s. In 2014 my wife and I visited the site of Fernlands, and we found that it had newly been cleared of all vegetation, exposing the concrete terrace wall to view for the first time in many decades. Later that year the site was redeveloped for an estate of thirteen new houses.

When in 2016 a friend proposed that together we join a local writing course, ideas that had been half-forming in my mind became, if I may use the word, more concrete, and this story began to take shape. Its premise, that Roman ruins had been incorporated into the fabric of the Victorian villa, also has its foundation in reality. Recently, archaeologists searching for Roman remains at a farm in Hampshire were baffled by the absence of physical evidence of buildings they knew to have existed – until they examined the concrete walls of farm buildings built in the 1870s. The rest of my story is supposition, exploring what might happen if the ancient world of Roman gods and goddesses collided with ours. I have moved Chertsey to a thinly-disguised Guildford, and Fernlands, now Ferndown, has moved to its outskirts, on the escarpment of the North Downs.

ACKNOWLEDGEMENTS

Many people have helped me bring this story to fruition. Without Susan Castillo Street's prompting I might never have started, and she has provided helpful support throughout; John Davies ably led our writing course and made many practical suggestions; from the Classics department at Tonbridge School Paul Parker introduced me to the world of Roman gods and Furies and Dr John Taylor, lecturer in Greek and Latin languages at Manchester University, translated lines from my English version of Juno's verse fragment into elegant Latin. My thanks also go to Melanie den Brinker, Mary James and my sister Jo Thom for their constructive comments. Finally I owe a debt of gratitude to my wife Carol and son Alex, both of whom have lived with concrete-related research for over a decade; Carol's contribution to this has been inestimable, as has her support as editor and proof-reader. And if I have taken liberties with the work (and the name) of Charles Drake I hope that, as my great-grandfather, he will forgive me.